Here I Stand

By Nicholas and Lauren Mazzio

Solemn Appeal Ministries
www.solemnappeal.com

Dedication

This book is dedicated to all who have chosen to stand
for Bible truth – no matter what the cost.

Contents:

Prologue

And they that shall be of thee shall build the old waste places: thou shalt raise up the foundations of many generations; and thou shalt be called, The repairer of the breach, The restorer of paths to dwell in. Isaiah 58:12

There are things that I had learned as a child that I never thought I would have to relearn as an adult. Simple things - like...standing.

When I was a kid, I was really afraid of storms. But when I look back on all that has happened to me over the short course of the last few months I realize something about storms that I never knew before. Storms bring us to God.

Gregory Martin

Chapter 1

~ The Underdog

A very expensive black Lincoln with darkened windows drove up the long, winding driveway to the main building of a modest private Christian college. The driver opened the door for the official looking visitors, one in shiny expensive leather Italian shoes who exited the car slowly, deliberately, followed by a man wearing cheaper, worn and scuffed shoes.

The man in scuffed shoes quickly jogged ahead to open the door to the college for his esteemed looking companion, and soon they were walking slowly and purposefully down the Hall of Graduates at the Martin Luther Bible College. The wearers of the shoes paused briefly as they looked at each of the pictures of the graduates, starting with the school's foundation year in 1879 to the present. The photo color and quality, as well as the hair styles of the graduates had changed with each passing year. The two men stopped abruptly and stood a long time in front of a gap in the line of photos where a picture and name plaque had obviously been removed leaving the glue remnants behind.

"Well, well. What happened here?" asked the man in the expensive shoes.

"It's a long story..." Embarrassed, the man in the scuffed shoes trailed off as he laughed uneasily.

"Really." Expressionless, the eyes of the man in the expensive shoes seemed to penetrate the hall, as if searching for secrets...

Outside, students milled about in a park-like recreation area of the campus they referred to as "the quad". Among the ones hanging out, soaking up the sun between classes were Gregory and Jeremy.

"I can't believe it - home stretch!" Gregory extended his legs out on the lawn as he clipped his laptop lid closed and leaned back on his book bag, basking in the warm spring breeze and sipping from his soda can.

"Nearly 4 years of torture and it all comes down to this..." Jeremy slipped his laptop into its case and zipped it closed.

"Torture? Has it really been that bad?" Gregory laughed and put his soda down in the grass.

"I guess it would depend on which class we were talking about!" Jeremy began cramming the garbage from their sandwich lunches into the brown paper bag the cafeteria had served them in. Professor Schwarzerd waived at him good naturedly as he walked over.

"Hey guys, going to miss you," he smiled.

"You haven't gotten rid of us yet, Professor Schwarzerd. We still have a few more months left." Gregory snuggled down into his book bag, looking more comfortable than ever.

Professor Schwarzerd shrugged as he smiled. "True. But I know you'll make it. Sola Gracia."

Jeremy snorted a laugh. "Yeah, you mean by the grace of our good professors!" He grabbed Gregory's soda can and added it to his growing bag of trash.

The professor smiled as he continued on his way. Jeremy watched him pensively, then hit Gregory on the shoulder. "Well, there's one professor I think I can say I will actually miss." Gregory opened a lazy eye to watch the professor as he stopped to give an encouraging word to another of his students in the quad.

"You mean almost miss - don't bask in freedom yet. We still have one more major hurdle before home stretch." He looked around for his soda, but

Jeremy had already tidied up the lunch mess. He grabbed the bag with the trash in it and started digging in it, eating some fries he found at the bottom of the bag.

"So, what are you going to write your final thesis on?" Jeremy asked.

"Ah, the thesis – the cap stone of the M.Div. The final mountain to climb - proving our worthiness to be called graduates of the great Martin Luther Seminary and College of Evangelism." Gregory smiled and crammed another fry in his mouth. Jeremy made a face as he noticed what Gregory was doing.

"Come on, seriously, we have to have our topics in by Friday."

Gregory dug his soda out of the trash bag, and wiping the edge of the can on his flannel shirt, took a sip before answering. "I don't know. It's a tough decision because I want it to be part of my resume package when I send out my applications for a call to pastor."

Jeremy snorted sarcastically, "Good idea! Send it with your resume so you can prove you can put people to sleep like any good pastor should!" He dodged a swipe from Gregory.

Just then, a very expensive car pulled up to the curb near the quad. A proper chauffeur opened the rear passenger door and a gentle looking student stepped out of the car. One couldn't help but notice a conscious air of kindness and power about him.

Gregory and Jeremy stopped to watch. He caught their eye and nodded a greeting as he disappeared toward his class.

"Isn't Fitz back a little late from break?" Jeremy said as he stood and swung his book bag over his shoulder. He tossed the garbage into the nearby trash can as he started walking toward his next class.

"Money can buy anything. Even at a Christian college. Seems like he comes and goes whenever he wants." Gregory finished off his soda, letting the last drips drop onto his tongue. "Must be nice to come from a rich and influential family." He took a shot toward the trash with his empty soda can and missed. The can bounced off the edge and spiraled onto the sidewalk. He shrugged and turned to walk toward his class.

Jeremy shook his head at his friend disapprovingly. Gregory feigned innocence. "You know what the king said, 'with great power comes great responsibility'." Jeremy said as he walked over to the can, picked it up, and tossed it into the nearby trash.

"And which king would that be?" Gregory asked.

"I don't know. But I'm sure one of them said it... because it's true."

"Well, those of us with no money or family influence actually have to work hard to impress people with our talent in order to get a call." Gregory walked quickly to catch up with his friend.

"Relax, you haven't even graduated yet." Jeremy answered offhandedly.

"Easy for you to say, you've already gotten three calls without sending out a resume, - and you haven't graduated yet either!"

Jeremy's shoulders slumped as he stopped short. "I feel like they just want a replica of my dad. You have no idea what it's like to have to live up to the towering shadow of three generations of successful pastors. Believe me, I'd rather be in your shoes than mine."

Gregory looked down at their shoes. His were worn, scuffed sneakers desperately needing replacement and Jeremy's were new-looking rich kid's shoes.

"Ok then, it's a deal. Let's trade shoes."

Jeremy looked down at their shoes and made a face. "Nice try."

The first bell sounded and they joined the rush of students jostling each other in the hall trying to reach their classes before the second bell signaled they were late.

Prophecy was one of the few classes they had together. In spite of Jeremy's best efforts, Gregory reached the door first, and grinned as he held it open for Jeremy. He walked through it impassively.

Dr. Ribera stood at the head of his senior prophecy class, not paying too much attention to the variety of student types in the room. Some were sleeping with their mp3 players on, others looked absently out the windows. He had a terrible habit of beginning his lectures early, in spite of the fact the majority of his students had to cross campus to reach his obscurely located classroom. He had insisted on the location because he liked the prestige of being in the new wing of the college. His students filed in noisily, trying to get settled and catch up on the class notes, but nothing fazed him as he carried on, undaunted.

"Remember, people are visual, so using charts is a very effective way to explain prophecies like the rapture and the end of time." He flipped open his laptop lid and began clicking with his mouse as the second bell sounded.

As his attention was diverted, a frazzled student tried to sneak into the class a little late. Dr. Ribera's cold stare stopped him short as he unexpectedly turned. "Late equals absent, Mr. Tibs."

The student gave a despairing, pleading look, but Dr. Ribera remained firm as he turned away and rattled on. "There are many pre-made charts available," he fired up his projector, "but I would encourage you to develop your own charts so you are very familiar and comfortable with them."

Jeremy was listening mildly. Gregory was listening intently and taking notes furiously, excited about what he was hearing. Jeremy smirked at his friend's customary over-enthusiasm.

Dr. Ribera continued, "Having your own charts also authenticates what you are saying, showing your congregants that you have studied these things for yourself." Dr. Ribera's projector flashed to life, shining his eschatology chart on the projection screen. "This is my chart – the one I like to use when explaining the prophecy of Daniel 9:24-27. Charts like these make it easy to show the two time periods in this prophecy - the 69 weeks that refer to the coming and ministry of the Messiah, which covers the time period from the decree to rebuild and restore Jerusalem after the captivity during the time of Daniel, all the way to Jesus' crucifixion. Then, in verse 27, regarding the 70th week, the prophecy changes focus and starts talking about the antichrist way down here at the end of time."

He suddenly became aware of the awkward silence around him as the classes' attention was riveted to a figure behind him. He followed their gaze toward Fitz, standing in the doorway. Their eyes met, and Dr. Ribera reluctantly nodded and gestured to a seat."Mr. Fitzgerald." Fitz nodded to Dr. Ribera as he took his seat.

Gregory raised his hand. "But how do we know that, Dr. Ribera? It kind of seems like one prophecy."

Off his rhythm, Dr. Ribera was irritated. "Know what, Mr. Gregory?"

Persistent, and seeking to ground his faith more firmly, Gregory poised his pen to add to his already lengthy notes. "How do we know that the prophecy is no longer talking about Jesus but the antichrist in verse 27?"

"It is an appropriate inferred change of direction, Mr. Gregory." Dr. Ribera gestured off-handedly as he turned to his time line again. "The main character of the plot changes. First, the focus is the coming of Christ, the Redeemer. At the close of time, the coming of the sinister antichrist takes center stage."

"But how do we *know* that, sir?" Gregory pressed persistently.

"Read the text, Mr. Gregory," Dr. Ribera answered sarcastically, "Do you honestly believe that the Messiah would destroy the city and the sanctuary and make it desolate?"

The class woke up a little and laughed. Fitz looked mildly at Gregory, who was blushing in embarrassment.

"No, sir. I just wanted to be able to explain it properly when the time comes. I've never really fully understood that part and I just wanted to know..." Gregory's voice started trailing as he sank down in his seat.

"Practice makes perfect." Noticing his discomfort, Dr. Ribera began coddling awkwardly, "You are too hard on yourself, Greg. Give yourself time to grow and develop your own style." He obviously struggled with giving encouragement. His hardened exterior didn't bend easily.

"But - " Gregory's attempt to explain his position was not permitted as the doctor continued, regarding the clock with more concern than he regarded his beleaguered student.

"Don't sweat it," Dr. Ribera rushed on a little too offhandedly, then caught himself, "When you're a pastor, everyone believes what you say anyway, even if you don't say it right. People will respect your teaching because of your title. Besides, everybody already knows this stuff. You'll be fine."

Trying to regain dignity, Gregory tried again, "But I want to be able to defend the prophecy - from the Bible."

Glancing at the clock again, Dr. Ribera began gathering his notes and wrapping up the class. "That's good," he was still too brusque. "Go study all the little ins and outs for yourself, but not on class time." Unable to restrain himself, he paused long enough to give Gregory a hard stare. "Aren't you graduating this year? This is just end of the year review. You should know all this by now."

"Yes, sir." Gregory shifted in his seat, even more embarrassed. The class snickered again as he looked around self consciously. Dr. Ribera flipped through his notes on his desk and looked at his watch in an annoyed manner. "Right, where were we? The mark of the beast. It is during this time of the seven years of tribulation that we believe the mark of the beast, the antichrist, appears, - because that's when the beast - the antichrist appears, here at the end of time. Now, we don't know exactly what the mark of the beast will be, but we know from Revelation 13 verses 16 and 17 that it goes on the hand or the forehead, and that without it nobody can buy or sell. So it's pretty serious stuff."

A buzzer sounded, indicating the end of class. Dr. Ribera sighed heavily. "That's all we have time for today, folks, see you next week. Please remember Friday is the deadline for you to email me your topic for your final thesis."

The students surged toward the door, pushing Gregory toward Jeremy as they made their way forward. "Why is it that every time I leave Dr. Ribera's class I feel like an idiot?"

"Practice makes perfect - you've been doing it all semester." Jeremy ribbed.

Gregory smirked at him sarcastically, "Oh, thanks for the encouragement, friend."

Chapter 2

~ The Long Story

The air in the college president's office was nearly as stuffy as the stoic decorum.

"Sir, your visitors are here," the ancient intercom system hissed with static in protest as it carried his Secretary Judy's equally aged voice into the president's office.

"Oh, wonderful," James Todd's voice cracked from the strain of his feigned, overly cheery voice. It betrayed his true sentiment as he cleared his throat. "Send them in, please, Judy."

He sighed deeply and ran his hand over his hair, smoothing a few loose strands in the reflection of one of the multiple monotonous degrees that burdened his walls. He practiced a smile. He looked tired and worn.

Judy graciously ushered the two guests from the hall of faith into James Todd's office.

"Pastor Irving! So good to see you again! Thank you for remembering your Alma Mater," James Todd smiled at the men and gestured to his plush seats nervously.

"Mr. Todd, I'd like you to meet Dr. Maitland, the newest addition to the sponsor board," Pastor Thomas Irving, the wearer of the worn shoes, bore a striking resemblance to the photo of a much younger Thomas Irving, only a few pictures down from the missing photo...

Even when seated at his massive desk with his extensive library lining the walls of his office behind him as if to back up his every word, James Todd felt especially vulnerable in front of his distinguished visitor. "Nice to meet you, Dr. Maitland," he shook hands with the doctor heartily and tried to keep his hand steady as he gestured toward a seat again.

"You too, Mr. Todd. How is the college?" Dr. Maitland's rich, sonorous voice was everything to be expected from one with such an imposing appearance.

"Splendid, splendid, still turning out some of the finest Christian minds of our time," James Todd's overenthusiastic smile was only mildly returned. He laughed nervously and continued uneasily, "We are sincerely grateful to God - and to your yearly grant - for keeping our doors open and our halls filled with bright, young Christians." He shifted uneasily in his seat in the short silence. A foreboding uneasiness began to creep over him as he watched Dr. Maitland's expressionless eyes taking in every detail of his office.

"I'm sure this will be just the normal routine visit we usually have," Pastor Irving tried to put the college president at ease. He always practiced a decided sensitivity that made him well liked. "Unless there is something special you want to point out to us - I'm sure the grant will be funded again."

"Thank you, Pastor Irving," James Todd eased back into his seat gratefully. "You know how much we rely on that grant to help us continue our work here."

"You're doing a good work here, James. The Schofield Society and the John Henry Newman Trust are happy and honored to support good Protestant Bible Colleges." Even though the words were reassuring, there was something about Dr. Maitland's tone, or was it his look - that made James Todd's forebodings return.

"And the Martin Luther Bible College *is* a good Protestant Bible college," James Todd hoped his demeanor came across more assertively than his voice and tone did. He hadn't meant it to be a question.

"Yes, it is, isn't it?" Dr. Maitland's tone was pensive.

James Todd tried to read Dr. Maitland as Pastor Irving thoughtfully surveyed the decorated walls. *Were they thinking of the missing graduate picture?*

"It's a good school, sir," James Todd squirmed in his big desk chair, feeling small. With all his heart he had wanted to avoid any controversial topics and now found himself feeling as if he were defending himself. "I stand by my graduates and their work." Sitting up a little straighter, he hoped his apparent firmness would end the question.

Dr. Maitland easily took control of the conversation with an air of unassumed authority. "I noticed there was a picture missing in your hall of faith."

"It's - it's a long story sir..." James Todd felt his color rising.

"Is it?" Dr. Maitland glanced at his watch mildly, then eased back into his chair and crossed his legs comfortably, indicating he had the time to listen. "Pastor Irving filled me in on some of the details while we were waiting. So sad to have a scandal like that come out of such a fine institution." James Todd squirmed once more in his seat under the doctor's steady stare. "But, I think you handled it well, considering the circumstances. Or we would have looked for a new college president." He laughed at his own joke, but James Todd had a hard time finding the humor in the remark as he shifted uncomfortably in his seat again. Silence blanketed the room like an icy realm ruled by Dr. Maitland alone. "Just see that it does not happen again." He leveled a meaningful stare at James Todd.

~

Just down the hall from that uncomfortable scene was a room filled with the antithesis of conflict.

Chalk dust floated lazily through the sunlight streaming through the window in Professor Schwarzerd's Sola Gracia class. It was located in the older section of the school, and the professor seemed to revel in it, even though he was offered a more modernized room. He wrote the final essay topic on his worn green chalk board - *"Sola Gracia, what this means to me."* The sound of pens, pencils and type pads filled the room as the students took notes around him.

"Psalm 85:10 - 'Mercy and truth are met together; righteousness and peace have kissed each other' - Where? At the cross," with his gentle and nurturing demeanor it was easy to see why he was so well liked. He continued with a touch of dramatic emphasis, "This will be your final essay for this class." A sigh of anticipation and muted excitement rippled through the room as he began handing back papers to his class, elementary school style. He didn't have to do it this way, but he obviously enjoyed the opportunity of closeness with his students. "Who can tell me the difference between the concepts of mercy and grace?" His gentle tone matched the kindness in his eyes.

"Grace is the opposite of works - Romans 11:6." An intrepid student ventured, his Bible open on his desk.

Professor Schwarzerd pondered the answer a moment. "Maybe too condensed. James says, 'I will show you my faith *by* my works' - yet he is, like all of us, saved by grace. His works did not annul grace. Anyone else? We're looking for a simple definition."

The class sat silently.

"Try to think of it in a way a child can understand." Every now and then he put a reassuring hand on a shoulder, and pat another on the back. "Remember, if you can reach up to the level of the understanding of children, you can ensure that you will encompass the minds of adults."

"Why is that reaching up?" a voice from the back interrupted.

"Jesus said, except ye be converted, and become as little children, ye shall not enter into the kingdom of heaven." Smiling, the Professor continued, "He set becoming as children as a goal for us to attain."

"I still don't get why He said that," Gregory said, intrigued at the reiteration of the familiar but not yet grasped concept, he stopped taking notes to listen.

"Ah, Mr. Gregory," Professor Schwarzerd started pacing slowly as he savored his favorite explanation, letting the words fall like water from his smiling lips, "It is because children are a fresh slate; they have nothing yet to re-write. They have no trouble understanding the most complex truths of salvation, because everything is still possible in their unjaded imaginations. Adults, on the other hand, have had years of failed dreams, dashed hopes, and searing disappointments. Jesus was constantly reminding the adults that all things are possible with Him. Children take that as a fact with God. After all, He is God. And God can do anything." He looked thoughtfully at his class, and then wrote "mercy" and "grace" in large capitals on the board.

"Simply put - Mercy is *not* receiving what you do deserve, and Grace *is* receiving what you don't." He perched himself on the edge of his desk as he surveyed the class, watching for reciprocation. "Give me an example."

"Me, getting an A in this class," a voice from the back joked as the class rippled with snickers.

Humored, the professor smiled and resumed his thoughtful pacing. "Ok - would that be mercy or grace?"

"Both." Jeremy quipped.

After the laughter died down, the professor took his place at the head of his class with a whimsical smile as he unfolded a story in the imaginations of his students.

"There was a wealthy slave owner during the time of the Civil War who was secretly buying slaves to

help them escape through the Underground
Railroad. One of his newly purchased slaves did
not really believe the rumors, and having suffered
so much at the hands of former slave owners he
was bent on causing his new owner as much pain
as possible. That night, he set fire to his master's
barn. He made it no secret that he was the culprit
either." Captivated by the story, his student's eyes
followed him around the room as he resumed his
thoughtful pacing. "Now, everyone knows you
can't just let something like that go. There has to be
punishment for bad behavior. Without law, there is
anarchy - and anarchy always harbingers death. To
maintain order, the slave owner called all the slaves
out to witness the punishment. The whip was
brought out, and the slave was asked to remove his
shirt. An almost universal gasp was heard as the
other slaves saw how his back was riddled with
scars from many previous beatings. Then the slave
owner took his own shirt off as well. The slave
about to receive the punishment was the one to
gasp now as he saw it was just as scarred as his
own. The slave owner spoke gently, 'We both
know what you did was wrong,' he said, 'and
punishment is due. But, I believe that things would
have been different if you had known me better.
So, this time, I will take your punishment, as Jesus
took mine, long ago on Calvary. Please, improve
on this opportunity and try doing better next time.'
Then he put the whip in the slave's hands and
stretched himself out on the whipping post, ready
to receive the beating. The whip fell to the ground
from the trembling slave's hand as the mercy and
grace shown him poured into his now broken
heart." His gentle smile radiated his joy as he

watched the impact of the truths he was presenting reflected on the faces of his students.

"But why not just let the slave get his punishment, and then set him free? He deserved it, didn't he?" A perplexed student asked.

"It was not enough to the slave owner for his new friends to be set free in this life," The Professor's meandering walk ended back at the head of his class. "He wanted them to be free, free indeed – in Christ. We too, are rightfully the property of God - first by creation, and second by redemption. He bought back His own, on the cross, but, like that slave owner, he bought us to set us free."

A brooding student raised his hand. The professor nodded for him to speak. "How do you know the slave won't just do it again?"

"Well... he might," The Professor paused, as he chose his words, "Freedom of choice is a right God has given to all His intelligent creatures. True love cannot be demanded. If it were, it would not be love. But, I believe that it is part of God's plan of salvation, His design and intent, that when a sinner truly sees himself standing at the bar of God, rightfully condemned, and then sees his beloved Saviour step into his place to take his punishment, a new realization is reached, and there is a new creature born of love. Truly, only God can create anew a heart dead in trespasses and sin."

"So, what's our part?" Jeremy's voice hesitatingly broke the quiet reverie, "Don't we do anything?"

"Yes, we have two very important responsibilities in our salvation." He paused for emphasis as he looked longingly at his beloved students, "One - to *let* God do this in us. Philippians 2:5 'Let this mind be in you, which was also in Christ Jesus. And two - we are to feed the new man. God lights the fire of love in our hearts, when we allow Him to, and then, with His grace and mercy, we allow Him, and work with Him, to keep it going." He savored the thoughtful silence, as though the world stood still a moment in awe of the concept. Then the moment was broken as the end of class bell rang.

Chapter 3

~ Inspiration Strikes

Jeremy put the book he was reading down and
sighed heavily as he glanced at the caller ID on his
ringing cell phone. He was trying to decide if he
would answer or not. He cast a measured look at
Gregory. He was sitting at his desk in front of his
computer, oblivious to the ringing phone as he
typed enthusiastically with his mp3 player on. On
his desk was a big note circled in the notebook
beside him "CREATE OWN VISUALS". Finally
at the last second, Jeremy flipped his cell phone
open, keeping a wary eye on Gregory to make sure
he couldn't be heard.

"Hi, Dad. How's Mom feeling?" Instinctively
Jeremy tried to lead the conversation away from
anything school related, "What did the doctor say?

...That's good. When can she go home?" He glanced at the family photo taped to his wall - his dad, the stalwart of the family, and his mom, small, twisted, and frail strapped to her little wheelchair. "... Ok. Tell her I love her. ..." He tried in vain to wrap the conversation up and keep it short, but then fell silent, as he listened to his dad's voice on the other side. Absently, only half paying attention, his finger traced the letters on a pile of religion text books. He pushed one of them over to reveal one very out of place - Aeronautics and Space. He traced the title as he continued talking on the phone absently, flatly. "...World religions eschatology... Yes, the test is on Tuesday....Oh, yeah - I'm studying hard for it, but... it's hard, you know. A lot of dates and Bible verses..." His voice trailed as he rolled his eyes at the familiar lecture on the other side.

Gregory stirred and startled him. He quickly buried the book under his pillow to hide it as he watched Gregory typing excitedly and pounding his head to the driving music he was listing to. He was clearly excited and into what he is doing on the computer, still, Jeremy regarded him cautiously.

"I know it was your favorite class," Jeremy's voice sounded more annoyed than he had meant it to be. Trying to be more respectful, he softened his tone, but it betrayed him and it came across more apathetic than respectful, "I'm - I'm just not very good at it. I just feel like my heart's not in it." He reached for his aeronautics book and paged through it in subconscious defiance as he listened in silence. He rolled his eyes at something his dad had said. Trying to restrain himself, he was a little short as he answered in a defeated, sing-song voice, "The heart is deceitful above all things and desperately wicked, yes, sir. I'll try my best to make you and grandpa proud." Tossing the book aside, he hung up, sighing deeply as he ran his fingers through his hair.

Suddenly Gregory tossed his ear buds onto the keyboard and stood up forcefully. The chair shot out from behind him and a startled Jeremy got the scare of his life.

"I've got it! Ha ha! I'm a perfect genius!" Gregory was talking loudly and excitedly.

"Argh! For crying out loud, Greg!" Jeremy was trying to regain his wits as he quickly covered his aeronautics books, "Why do you always have to *do* that!?"

"What? What did I do?" Gregory was oblivious as he stared at his frazzled friend. Jeremy blew his cheeks out and regained his composure.

"You'd think after all these years I'd get used to it right?" Jeremy scolded himself quietly.

"The Mark of the Beast!" Gregory shouted triumphantly.

Uninspired, Jeremy turned back to one of his theology books, only half listening, "What about it?"

"No one knows what it is!" Undaunted, Gregory carried on his glorious enthusiasm.

"Yes. And?" Jeremy stared at him, annoyed and impatient.

"I'm going to find out - study it out in the Bible - and *prove* what it is. And that, my friend, is how I will *finally* leave Dr. Ribera's class with dignity for once." Gregory's resolute exuberance evoked a much less inspired response in his roommate's amused expression. "This is going to be the most incredible thesis this college has ever seen! They may even put my picture in the hall of fame next to yours - and your dad's and granddad's and great-granddad's, old Mr. James Gray himself!"

"Please! Don't remind me!" Jeremy rolled over in his bed and covered his head with a pillow.

"It must be so incredible, Jer -" Gregory stretched himself out on his bed, hands cradling his head as he stared at the ceiling, too excited to notice his friend's palpable distress.

Jeremy's muffled voice penetrated the pillow, "What?"

"To be you. To actually have the same blood coursing through your veins as the Great James Gray - who was one of the original seven editors of the first Scofield Study Bible. Incredible. You are so blessed."

Jeremy shoots an unnoticed look of incredulity at his friend from behind the pillow. "Sure, you have no idea. Whatsoever." Jeremy retorted sarcastically as he dramatically buried his head back under his pillow.

~

With a new air of confidence, Gregory strode into Dr. Ribera's classroom and respectfully dropped a typed page onto the Professor's desk. Dr. Ribera picked up the paper and scrutinized it with an amused smile.

"What's this, Mr. Gregory?" Dr. Ribera read from the typed page, " 'The Mark of the Beast'... interesting. I didn't know you were into technology. This should be...entertaining."

Jeremy took in the scene quietly from over his friend's shoulder and shook his head, "Uh oh, that's not good, Greg."

"Sir, it's not meant to be entertaining," Gregory's enthusiasm was unabated, "it's meant to be - apocalyptic! Mind blowing! Profound!"

Dr. Ribera put the paper disinterestedly onto the stack on his desk and smiled mildly, "Yes. Well, we'll see, won't we?"

Fitz was next in line to turn in his topic. He raised his eyebrows, intrigued, as he glanced at Gregory's topic sitting on the top of the pile of papers on Dr. Ribera's desk. "Interesting topic," Fitz said quietly. He nodded to Gregory as he and Jeremy made their way to their seats.

"Yes, well, sometimes a boy can choke when he bites off more than he can chew," Dr. Ribera smirked, snatching Fitz's paper from him in annoyance.

Just then Fitz's phone went off as he received a text message. Quickly reading it he nodded to Dr. Ribera. "Can you email me the notes for today's lecture please?" Without waiting for a response, he turned, already dialing and strode out of the class talking quietly into his phone. "Yes, sir. I'll be on the curb waiting."

Just outside Dr. Ribera's classroom window, James Todd was escorting his guests to their waiting car.

"Thank you, gentlemen, for the visit. I really hope you enjoyed your stay in our newly updated guest house." James Todd was still eager to somehow gain the approbation of Dr. Maitland as he opened the car door for him. "We hope having such nice quarters to offer the families of our visiting prospective students would encourage the attendance of more influential and... well-off families, if that is alright to say."

"It's not a curse to have money, or to attract those with money, Mr. Todd." Dr. Maitland chided, "Nicodemus did much to support the work *because* he had means."

"Yes. Well, it does help." Pastor Irving tried to lighten the discourse with his soft laugh. James Todd cleared his throat nervously.

An expensive looking car pulled up to the curb for Fitz who stepped up to the curb a few feet behind their car. James Todd caught his eye and waved obsequiously. Fitz gave a small, uncomfortable wave back, expressionless, and got into the car. It pulled away sharply. James Todd turned his attention back to his guests. Dr. Maitland looked questioningly at James Todd.

"Oh, we try to accommodate the needs of some of our more influential students and their families." James Todd's flagrant toadyishness was even beginning to get on Pastor Irving's nerves as he suppressed a comment.

Dr. Maitland paused, pondering thoughtfully a moment, then answered, "Sounds...sycophantically wise of you." James Todd's face registers momentary confusion as he tried to read if that was a compliment or not. Dr. Maitland did not give him the satisfaction of a conclusion as he continued, "We had a fine time and a good stay. The college has grown, appears to be theologically sound and still in accordance with our teaching. After the final review, I'm sure the funding will continue."

"Final review? Is this something new?" James Todd's uneasiness returned again full force as he shifted uneasily from foot to foot in the cold wind.

"Yes, a bulletin was sent to...certain sponsored colleges," Pastor Irving compassionately tried to ease his mind.

"A random sampling of your seminary students' thesis papers will be taken to a review board." Dr. Maitland's sonorous and authoritative voice made everything he said sound even more imposing than the words themselves.

Pastor Irving shrugged sympathetically, "One of our major donors now requires we ensure the teachings are kept to our standard by reviewing the student's thesis papers."

"Oh." It wasn't much of a response, but all that James Todd could manage as he tried to phrase his next words in such a way that would ask what he needed to know without unnecessarily exposing himself to the scrutiny he so desperately wanted to avoid. He tried to sound nonchalant and surprised as he continued mildly, "Our little college was one of the ones picked for review?"

"I think it appropriate." Dr. Maitland's demeanor conveyed that he was not to be trifled with as he stared steadily back at him, "Though you handled the situation well, and we don't judge the whole barrel on the performance of one 'bad apple', of course." James Todd's expression betrayed his concern as Dr. Maitland continued critically, "Just a word of advice in these troubled financial times though, Mr. Todd. There are many colleges looking for sponsorship, as I am sure you know. So, try your best to weed out the trouble makers before they graduate. It makes all of our jobs a lot easier, don't you think?"

James Todd's expression betrayed his concealed distress. Pastor Irving slapped him heartily on the back, "Well, don't look so down, man! Spelling and grammar aside, I'm sure your students will do fine! Don't worry so much."

"You'll be hearing from us next month." Dr. Maitland stated matter-of-factly, "Please make sure to send us your students' topics as soon as possible so we can choose a few to review."

"All the students? All the theology classes?" Overwhelmed at the thought, James Todd struggled to keep his composure, "That's a lot of classes!"

Considering his point, Pastor Irving laughed, "No, of course not all! We have so many schools to go through, that would be far too many papers! Just a sampling from one final year class will be just fine."

"Well, which class then?" He looked expectantly at the men. Dr. Maitland and Pastor Irving looked at each other a moment. They had not discussed which class. It hadn't mattered. They shrugged at each other and Dr. Maitland shook his head to mean it didn't really matter to him. Pastor Irving shrugged and answered, "How about prophecy?"

Chapter 4

~ Providential Interventions

Gregory was over-loading the dryer with his wet clothes as he preached into the air passionately. "So, dear brethren,...brethren and sisters - brothers...and sisters, the word 'rapture' doesn't actually appear in the Bible, but the idea comes from Thessalonians 4:17 where Paul writes that 'we which are alive and remain shall be caught up to meet Him in the air.' ... are you with me? Good."

He didn't notice, but a pretty, young girl about his age began watching him as she folded clothes on a table nearby, amused by his oblivious enthusiasm as he continued preaching. "And when does that happen? In 2 Peter 3:10, the Bible says - Peter says - that's why it's called 2 Peter, because Peter wrote it," He dropped a white tee shirt on the floor, but did not notice as he continued preaching, "So, Peter says, wait - I mean the Holy Spirit through Peter says - because all Scripture is given by the inspiration of the Holy Spirit - and inspiration' means 'breathed', like you 'in-spire' and 'ex-pire' – like, breathe your last..." He breathed in and out deeply as he illustrated his point, "...anyway, Peter says in 3:10, 'Jesus will come as a thief in the night.' So, that must mean He must be coming secretly, right? Right."

He unconsciously stepped on the wet white tee shirt and dragged it across the very dirty laundromat floor, leaving the shirt very dirty. His unseen watcher giggled, unnoticed. "So, using these two verses we understand that He comes secretly and raptures all His believers away. After this, the antichrist comes, and for 7 years there is trouble on earth, because then he forces his mark on everyone." He finally felt a lump under his foot and noticed the dirty shirt lying at his feet. He picked it up and surveyed the damage a moment. Then, giving it a little shake and a ceremonial wipe on his pant leg, he tossed it in with the rest of his clean clothes. She rolled her eyes laughing. "Anyway, so, now you know what the Bible says about the rapture. But that's not really what this sermon is about - it's about the mark of the beast! Just wait until I explain to you what that is! And I will- ... as soon as I figure out what it is." He slammed the door, punctuating his sermon.

Digging in his pocket, he tossed 4 quarters into the machine and then pressed the button. Nothing happened. He put his hands on his hips and stared at the coin slot. "How do you start this thing?" He looked up at the newly painted sign over on the wall advertising the newly installed dryers and sighed to himself as he started hunting for some type of instruction or clue as to how to make them work. His silent, giggling, smiling congregant came to his rescue. "Oh, hey. I was just ready to start this thing," he pointed at the unresponsive machine. "It ate my quarters, but..." She smiled and laughed lightly as she turned the knob that chose the heat setting and pressed the button. The machine churned to life. Gregory gave her a sheepish look of thanks as she turned and smiled at him.

"That was some sermon. I think you have a convert."

"You!?" Gregory was unable to contain his excitement as he ran his fingers through his hair, unable to find words to continue, but his giggling rescuer looked over at a cute little girl gazing at the toys in the quarter machines.

"No, her," she made eye contact and the giggling little girl came running, throwing her little arms around her leg. She laughed good naturedly and looked down lovingly at the little girl clinging to her leg.

The little girl turned her big brown eyes on Gregory and said cutely, "you're funny."

"Well, that's a good start, isn't it?" Gregory smiled back.

"Yeah, it is," his smiling new friend dragged a

clothes cart over to a machine that had just ended its drying cycle and began unloading the clothes into it as she talked, "but I think you're going to have a hard time figuring out that 'mark of the beast' thing, without knowing who the beast is, anyway."

Gregory's face registered his surprise. "Really? What do you mean? The beast is the antichrist right? What did I do wrong?"

She sized him up, noting the insignia and crest on his laundry bag. "You're a seminary student at the Martin Luther Bible College, right?"

"Yes..."

"Well, you know what the Reformation is, right?"

"Yes. Um...well, kind of. Ok, no."

"So... then you've probably never heard of the counter-Reformation either, right?"

"Counter-Reformation?"

The gruff owner of the laundromat briskly exited the back room into the main laundry area, eying her sourly. She glanced over nervously and started pushing the loaded cart to her table as the little girl ducked behind the clothes with a mock frightened face.

"Look, I've got to fold these clothes. Maybe we can talk another time? Ok?" She smiled warmly as she loaded the clothes onto the table.

Gregory stumbled over his words, wishing they could keep talking. "Ok. Thanks for the help on - with the machine." Gregory grabbed his empty laundry bag and started to head toward the door. "And I'd really like to hear more about the beast thing..."

She beamed another big smile at him as she continued folding. "Ok."

"Ok." Gregory smiled back. The little girl under the table wiggled her cute little fingers at him in a wave as he nearly tripped out the door walking backwards. They both giggled at him. His smile transformed into a big goofy grin as he turned and walked out the door.

~

Gregory grabbed an over-stuffed sub at the cafeteria, then spied Jeremy sitting at a booth alone surrounded by a fresh order of French fries, fried chicken fingers, and fried onion rings. His head was bopping to his mp3 player, and his aeronautics books were sprawled across the table. Stealthily Gregory sneaked up unnoticed, then bounced over the bench seat and landed across the table from Jeremy, scaring him witless again as he suddenly landed in the booth.

"Hey, Jer!" Gregory yelled as he landed.

Jeremy gasped like a goldfish, slamming his books shut and quickly placing the seminary titles over the science titles as Gregory stole an onion ring and crammed it into his mouth.

"Are you *trying* to kill me before the school year is over?" Jeremy's exasperation gave his tone a whining quality that gave fuel to Gregory's pleasure at the success of his ambush.

"You should be used to it by now. Besides, you're too easy to scare. You make it so much fun." Gregory stole another onion ring and crammed it into his mouth. "You know, you shouldn't be eating all this fried food. It's not good for you." Jeremy looked at him, then at Greg's untouched sandwich, and then watched another of his onion rings and a handful of his fries disappear into his friend's mouth.

"You don't say." Retorted Jeremy flatly as he started gathering his things with mild annoyance.

"Seriously, I need help." Gregory used a couple French fries as chopsticks to try to lift a ketchup laden onion ring to his mouth.

"I know that." Jeremy answered again flatly as he watched the onion ring land on the table.

"No, really," Gregory pleaded, a little distracted as he tried again.

"Really. I know." Jeremy sighed and started sliding his books into his backpack.

"It's this girl I met in the laundromat -" Gregory was talking with his mouth full.
"What!? You know the rules, no girls, no dating on or off campus! Instant expulsion with no refund!" Suddenly aware of how loud he is speaking,

Jeremy gave a furtive glance around at who might have heard him then hushed his tone and continued, "This is a girl-free zone! I'm surprised they don't have 'no girls allowed' signs everywhere, you know! Remember that 'agreement' they had us sign at enrollment - they mean it. Don't even think about dating. Why do you think there aren't that many girls enrolled here? You know they all go to school to get their MRS."

"MRS? I don't follow you." Gregory stared uncomprehendingly at him.

"Their 'Mrs.'?! You committed to being committed to God during your schooling, and God only. Another few months and you'll be home free, but for now, play it safe."

Suddenly comprehending, Gregory answered defensively, "No, I don't think it's like that -"

"Of course not, what could she see in you anyway?" Jeremy ribbed.

"Ha ha. No. Listen, I was preaching about the end of the world and she said I had the part about the beast wrong. But she didn't tell me what I had wrong. The beast is the Antichrist, right?" Gregory was gesturing with a ketchup laden onion ring.

Jeremy shrugged disinterestedly, "Sounds about right. Wait a minute - who were you preaching to? I thought you were at the laundromat."
"I was - was preaching to...no one - to the machines, ok? I 'air preach' sometimes, ok?"

Jeremy smirked at him, unable to refrain himself, "Air preach? Is that like air-guitar or something? Only way less cool?"

"Come on, what do you think?" Gregory looked pleadingly at his friend.

Jeremy gave it a scholarly thought, then answered, "The beast, the antichrist, the man of sin - they are all figures the Bible uses to describe the same person. How can they be anything else?"

"Ok. So then, what am I missing? Conviction? Scripture? Presence?" Gregory continued cramming fries and onion rings as he pondered his own questions.

"I don't know, I wasn't there. Go ask her." Jeremy gathered his things and stood to leave with his usual air of perpetual annoyance.

"That's a good idea. I think I will. I think she works there."

"Just don't get caught with her and give someone the wrong impression..." As a last thought before leaving, Jeremy grabbed Gregory's sandwich and started walking down the hall, nearly running into Dean Bellarmine.

"Don't get caught with 'her'?" The dean glowered at Jeremy suspiciously as Jeremy is caught of guard.

"Oh, Dean Bellarmine, sorry sir, I didn't see you."

"I'm *always* watching son. You should be too." The dean eyed Jeremy with another surly look.

"Ye - yes, sir."

Shooting a look of disdain at both of the young men, the dean continued on his way down the hall. Jeremy glared at Gregory. Gregory, feeling his innocence, offered him some fries dipped in ketchup. Jeremy turned away and continued down the crowded hall. Gregory noticed something on the seat beside him. One of Jeremy's books had fallen off the table in his haste to cover them up. He picked it up and stared at the cover, then read it out loud to himself, "The Science of Flight. Aerodynamics, Propulsion, Materials and Structures, Stability and Control." He looked at his friend's retreating figure disappearing down the hall. 'Well, what do you know, Pastor Jeremy?"

~

Later that evening, the same pretty girl Gregory had talked to earlier sighed tiredly and stretched her back as she continued folding clothes at her table. She was watching over the little girl sleeping on a warm pile of laundry nearby.

Outside the glass doors behind her, a rowdy group of college guys from the nearby Martin Luther Bible College eyed her shapely figure eagerly, each daring the other to go talk to her. Finally they mustered up enough mob courage and entered the laundromat like a pack of hungry dogs, laughing incongruously as they pushed and shoved each other into a hierarchy. Startled from sleep, the little girl roused from her warm bed of clothing and then hid under the nearest table.

The leader of the group sauntered over to the pretty girl as she continued folding, as if oblivious. He dropped his book bag loudly on the nearby seat. The college's insignia was prominently embroidered on his shirt and his bag. Spurred on by the other boys' eager eyes, he leaned over the table forwardly into her personal space. But her jaw was set as she continued to ignore him. His cronies laughed at his failed attempt, egging him on. He watched her with eager suggestiveness, letting his eyes play over her body lasciviously.

"Hey, baby, let's go fold some laundry together," he imagined himself smooth as he looked back at his friends.

Impassive, she loaded her arms with folded clothes and started walking away from him toward the back of the laundromat, brushing past him as if he didn't exist. He looked at her expectantly until she passed, then, realizing she was spurning him, he shot an angry look after her as she disappeared into the back room.

Frustrated and embarrassed as his friends rolled over each other, laughing, he punched the table with his fist, making the unseen little girl underneath jump, wide eyed and frightened. Finally he grabbed his bag and led his cronies out the door.

Shortly, the pretty girl returned to her folding table and kept folding. The little girl under the table watched the door where they went out with concern in her eyes.

In a dark corner of the laundromat, Dean Bellarmine folded his clothes quietly, surveying the scene in silence.

Chapter 5

~ The Beginning

Martin Luther's Study 1516

Martin Luther sat at his writing desk wrapped in a blanket, and wrote with a quill and ink by candlelight.

My Dear Spalatin, We cannot attain to the understanding of Scripture either by study or strength of intellect. Therefore your first duty must be to begin with prayer. Entreat the Lord to deign to grant you, in his rich mercy, rightly to understand His word. There is no other interpreter of the word but the Author of that word Himself. Hope nothing from your study and strength of intellect; but simply put your trust in God, and in the guidance of His Spirit. Believe one who has made trial of this matter.

Gregory turned the page of an ornately embellished, worn, leather-bound book on the Reformation as he lay in bed, reading. There was a large stack of others beside his bed.

~

It was cold outside the laundromat as Gregory walked up to the window eagerly, note pad in hand. He looked through the glass window for his pretty friend. Relieved, he smiled as he saw her folding clothes at a nearby table. He swung a large bag of laundry over his shoulder and walked through the door, passing the little girl sitting on the floor gazing at a little monkey in the quarter toy machine.

"Hi, I'm ready to try again." Gregory smiled as he dropped his bag into a cart. She didn't look up, but smiled slightly. "You - you remember me, right?" A hint of despair crept into Gregory's tone as he wheeled his cart over so she could see his face.

"How could I forget?" She didn't look up from her work as she answered, "The guy that likes to preach to dryers... or is it to the clothes, right sweetie?" She smiled down at the little girl who wandered over and giggled at their little inside joke.

"She's so cute. Is she your niece or little sister?" Gregory returned the shy wave he received. Finally the girl stopped folding.

"She's my daughter." She lifted her chin, smiling deliberately, but ready for the usual condescension.

"Whoa. I - I didn't know. Sorry. Wow." He looked at the cute little girl as he apologized.

"I'm not."

"Not what?"

"Sorry. She's great. She's my blessing." The little girl smiled at her mom who smiled back. Gregory stood awkwardly not knowing how to recover from his flub. Graciously his uneasiness was noticed. "So, what can I do for you? That looks about 25 pounds of dirty laundry... They charge by the pound, you know."

"No. No - I didn't know that, and no, you don't have to do it. I'll do it. I just wanted to talk to you." He shook his head to clear the horrible thought from his mind of this pretty girl washing his crusty socks.

"...So you saved up all your laundry?"

"Yeah, kind of," Gregory shrugged sheepishly, "I'm down to my last pair of jeans. Ran out of clean shirts yesterday... We're not supposed to be seeing girls while at seminary. Supposed to keep focused, you know."

"No, actually I'd never know." Her mind filled with the memory of the students from the other night. Suddenly cold, his new friend turned away. "Look, you don't have to waste your time, you're not my type and besides, I'm not 'on the market.' My heart's taken, right sweetie?" She cast a significant smile to the little girl who smiled back.

"No - no," Gregory retreated hastily, "that came out all wrong. I'm not here to see you, I just want to talk to you...without seeing you - I mean I don't want to see you, though I do see you, I mean, you're right there, it's just - I just want to talk. That's all." She raised her eyebrows in disbelief as she walked away from him toward her folding table. Gregory followed her, anxious that he had lost his opportunity. "...about my sermon, about the rapture, the Reformation, the beast... about what you said, remember? I've been reading up on the Reformation... amazing!"

She stared blankly at him. "I'm busy. I'm sorry I can't help you."

"You know, one thing that is seriously missing in my college career is practice with real people." The sound of Gregory's sincere desperation halted her in her tracks.

"So, you want to... practice on me? Is that it?" She replied sarcastically. "I thought you were a seminary student, now you're trying to be like a doctor or a lawyer or something?" She turned to face him, amused again.

"Well, I hope to be a doctor...of divinity... someday." Undaunted by her jibe, Gregory replied, "I just really want to serve the Lord. And I felt like you were listening...the other day when I was sort of, you know, 'air preaching'." His shyness and absolutely transparent vulnerability was disarming.

"Air preaching?" She sized him up again. "Never heard that one before. You're not very good at it, are you?"

"I'd like to be." Feigning hurt, Gregory kidded defensively. "I'd like some honest feedback. I felt like that was what you gave me. I appreciated it..." He stood awkwardly a moment as she stared at him, weighing his words and reading his face as he squirmed under her stare. "Can we start over?"

She shrugged at the little girl who smiled at her cutely, then looked expectantly back at Gregory.

"So, what's your name?" She tilted her head to the side as if the answer would determine her decision. He squirmed.

"Gregory. - Um, Greg."

She stuck out her hand for a handshake. "Well, 'Pastor Um Greg', I'm Melanie, and this is my daughter, Missy."

Greg fumbled with his laundry bag awkwardly, trying to get a hand free to shake. "Melanie. Nice to meet you. Thanks. Hi, Missy. Do you like monkeys?" Missy nodded at him, smiling. "Me too." He smiled back.

Melanie's boss walked briskly through to the back room, glaring at her as he passed.

"Um, I'm going to lose my job if I don't fold and talk, though. You mind?" She pushed a loaded cart toward an open table.

"No! No, not at all. Please, fold. I'll just toss these things into a machine... and be right back." He headed toward the machines with his large bag.

"Ok. But don't overload it though. The clothes don't come out as clean." Greg smiled back at her over his shoulder at the friendly tip.

~

Professor Schwarzerd wrote "Sola Gracia" on the white board then began handing back his student's papers.

"Sola Gracia. Salvation is by grace alone. Seems so simple, yet we can make it so complex." He looked down at a sleeping student and placed his paper gently on his head so as not to disturb him, then motioned for the class to stay quiet as they snickered. "Most of you did very well on the essay - I have marked some areas where I would like to see improvement. Considering your current end of the year work load, and because this is the *only* course on the important topic of grace you will take during your studies here, I have decided to give you an experience in grace to help you understand the concept. I have extended the deadline for your final essay two weeks."

A wave of quiet enthusiasm rippled through the class, waking the sleeping student as his paper fell from his head.

"Can you do the same thing for our Biology final?" Someone called from the back.

The professor smiled and shook his head.

"Why *did* you decide to teach both this Gospel and Grace class and Biology?"

"Small schools have big needs." Another voice answered.

"In other words: it's cheaper than hiring another teacher?" Gregory quipped as the class rippled with laughter.

The professor waited until the laughter died down and answered, "Actually, it's because I thought biology had a lot to do with grace. I felt they went hand in hand."

"How you came to that conclusion is a mystery to me!" Jeremy said loudly under his breath as more laughter came from the students.

The professor smiled and elaborated, "Well, just as biology shows that all creation is the handiwork of God, Grace shows that all conversion, the making of a new man with new likes and impulses - is no less an act of creation than creating the world." He let the class ponder his words a moment as he returned to his seat behind his overflowing desk. The spirit of joviality still hovered in the room.

"You know what I want to know? What do calculus and biology have to do with winning souls for Christ?" The sleepy student said as he stretched and joined the banter. "Why do pastors have to take those classes anyway?"

"I guess they wanted to make sure you know the difference between the species so you don't waste time preaching to the wrong life form - and they wanted to make sure you can count the baptisms!" Jeremy answered smartly as another wave of laughter ran through the class.

"Wise guy! You have an answer for everything." Gregory smiled as he punched his friend in the shoulder playfully.

~

Later, in a rare moment of seclusion, Jeremy found himself sitting in one of the plush chairs in the dorm lounge alone, with a soda in hand and his feet comfortably crossed on the coffee table, surrounded by a pile of his beloved flight magazines. He sighed deeply with his eyes half closed, as if feeling relief at the indulgence of undisturbed pleasure with his passion as he paged through one of the magazines, studying the planes, soaking in the flight stories. Then suddenly, like an undercover enemy spy, his cell phone rang, breaking his reverie. Glancing at it with disdain, he noted the familiar number and battled the temptation to ignore the call. Once again, at the last second, he flipped it open, self-consciously covering the magazines with a seminary book, even though the caller obviously couldn't see them.

"Hey, Dad. What's up?" He tried to sound cheerful, but it still came across annoyed. Always being in

the reach of his father's voice was like constantly
being haunted by an accusing presence from which
he felt he could never escape. This was actually the
fourth cell phone he had that year. For some
reason, they kept getting lost...or breaking
somehow.

"Hey, son. How is the paper going?"

*Was that an overt accusation? Or just a way to
start a conversation? Why do I always have to
analyze every conversation? Why can't I just say
"hi" like a normal person?* "It's going. I have a few
weeks to go yet." Jeremy's thoughts made his tone
uncontrollably defensive.

"What is that supposed to mean? Did you pick a
topic yet?" *Another accusation? Or was that a
legitimate question considering the cost of a four
year college degree?*

"Of course! They were due last week..." Jeremy
felt panic rising as his perceived interrogation
continued.

"So? What is it?" He tried to imagine his dad's
smiling face and stop feeling he was under
examination, but all he could hear was the
demanding tone, all he could feel was the
pressure...real or imagined - he couldn't ever tell.
He sat up and rubbed his forehead, trying to clear
the airplanes out of his mind, trying to remember.
"It's uh - it's about -" A long pause followed...too
long.
"Jeremy! This is the most important thing in your
life!" Jeremy's dad's tone was now unmistakably

stern. "Don't tell me you can't even remember your topic! You're supposed to be working on it, soaking in it, bending every cell in your brain to show the college you know your stuff!" Jeremy's conscience joined in the accusation as his face crumpled in depression. "Probably got your head stuck in some flight magazine. Waste of time..." His dad muttered under his breath.

Jeremy's jaw clenched as he looked at his piles of flight magazines. How could his dad see them from so far away? He felt his control failing as his emotions raged to consume him. "I know, I know! Look, I'm just not you, ok? I don't get it! I don't get how you just keep taking it from a God who just stands there and watches Mom suffer when He could do something about it!" He spat the words out as the feelings he has held back for so long threatened to engulf him.

"Son, it's not for us to know the purposes of the Almighty." His father's practiced preachy tone grated against his brittle nerves. "Sometimes you've just got to trust. And keep hoping. For hope maketh not ashamed."

"Easy for you to say, but I don't feel that way, ok? I need something that makes sense!" Tears welled in his eyes like writhing, seething floodwaters pounding against a shuddering dam.

"Like science? As if science is predictable?" There was no mistaking the accusing and ridiculing tone in his father's voice now. "You hide in the theories and the laws of flight as if they are going to shield you from a crash. Well, they won't you know, people die in airplanes and spaceships and hang gliders - no matter what the theory of flight says. Son, the only constant we have is God. You need to stop fighting Him and let go. God is in control. So you don't need to be."

A rebellious, silent, angry tear escaped Jeremy's eye. He silently punched the couch and threw one of his magazines across the room as he fought to keep the rest of the dam in place.

"Son?" His father's voice, now softer, reached out into the silence on the other end of the line. Jeremy bit his teeth into his fist to keep from crying out loud as his dad strained to hear in the stillness. He sighed. "Your mother sends her love... She said to tell you she is praying for you... We love you son. Talk to you later."

Jeremy closed his cell phone and tossed it onto the couch as he ran his fingers through his hair, exhaling deeply and leaning hard into the cushions behind him. The tears now streamed unchecked down his face as he looked upward.

"Why, God?" He breathed softly at the ceiling. "Why!" The escaping sound of his raging roar echoed unanswered down the empty hall as he brandished his fist at the ceiling, sobbing and then angrily sending the rest of the magazines crashing to the floor with another powerful swing of his clenched fist.

Chapter 6

~ Light in the Darkness

The afternoon sunlight was streaming through the streaky glass windows of the laundromat where Gregory and Melanie were at folding tables across from each other, each working on folding large piles of clothing. Missy was busying herself, studying the toy vending machines. The illusive little monkey figurine peeked teasingly at her from behind the glass with a crooked smile. But there were also a lot of other figurines that might come out if a quarter were put in, and none of them were as nice. It was the only monkey in the whole machine. She tapped the glass and returned the crooked smile, imagining that they were somehow communicating.

"So, that's my sermon on the rapture. What do you

think?" Gregory finished folding his last piece of laundry and put it on top of his pile.

"People vanishing? Cars crashing? Clothing lying on the floor? Seems like a sad world with all the kids gone." Melanie started loading her folded piles into bags as she glanced protectively at Missy.

"Yes. It is definitely sad. But, God is giving a second chance to their parents who are left behind, you know. Because He is merciful." He pensively packed his clean clothes into his sack.

"Really." Melanie's tone was surprised. "Is that how you see it?"

"Yeah, I do. What? You don't think He's merciful?"

"Oh, no, He's very merciful. I just don't think it's going to happen like that."

"Really? Then how is it going to happen? Or don't you think it's going to happen?"

"Oh, it's going to happen," Melanie smiled, "just not like that."

"How can you be so sure?"

"Because I read my Bible, and that's not what it says." She picked up the stack of clothes she had been folding and headed toward the back with it. Gregory swung his sack of clean laundry over his shoulder and jogged after her.

"What? Wait! What do you mean?"

"You're the seminary guy, what does your Bible say?"

"I just told you, the rapture, the antichrist, the whole deal." He jogged after her and opened the door to the back room for her.

"No, that's what your *professors* say. What does your *Bible* say? Look at it with fresh eyes and let me know what you see."

"Fresh eyes?" Gregory looked back at her blankly.

"Your own eyes. Not someone else's. Try reading it without any preconceived ideas, like a little child reading a story for the first time." She dropped the bags of fresh clothes in the rack for pickup and grabbed another large bag of dirty clothes to wash.

"Ok. I'll try. But I'd like to hear what you think too."

"Ok. Next time." She turned toward a machine and started filling it busily under the glaring, watching eyes of her surly employer.

"Ok. Next time." He tossed his bag over his shoulder with a smile and gathered his things as he turned to go.

"Hey, Martin Luther Bible College guy - try starting with studying Martin Luther, ok?"

"Is that a hint?"
"Maybe." She disappeared into the back with a smile.

~

Except for the soft clicking of incessant typing coming from one lone computer, the college library was silent that night. Gregory was alone, but busy. He referred often to several large reference volumes and books that were scattered around him as he searched the electronic archives and copied large sections of material to his flash drive. All the while he was typing, his mind piecing together an ancient puzzle in living history.

As Martin Luther, with noble firmness, stood in defense of the gospel, his doctrines spread, and priests and people rallied about him as their standard-bearer. Hard as it was for them to change their opinions, the light of truth was dispelling the darkness of error.

A new emperor, Charles V., had ascended the throne of Germany, and the emissaries of Rome hastened to present their congratulations, and induce the monarch to employ his power against the Reformation. On the other hand, the Elector of Saxony, to whom Charles was in great degree indebted for his crown, entreated him to take no step against Luther until he should have granted him a hearing. The emperor was thus placed in a position of great perplexity and embarrassment. The papists would be satisfied with nothing short of an imperial edict sentencing Luther to death. The elector had declared firmly that neither his imperial majesty nor anyone else had yet made it appear to him that the reformer's writings had been refuted; therefore he requested that Doctor Luther be furnished with a safe-conduct, so that he might answer for himself before a tribunal of learned, pious, and impartial judges. In the hearts of those who would obey his word, the Lord placed a firmness and decision that nothing could move.

~

With his escorts, a tired and way worn Martin Luther stopped beneath a tree on his way to Worms to drink and refresh themselves.

"This is where we must part, Melanchthon." Luther turned to his young friend with firmness.

"No, Martin, I cannot leave you! Especially in this hour of great trial." Grasping Luther's shoulders, the younger man clung firmly to his friend.

"If I do not return, and my enemies put me to death at Worms, continue to teach, and stand fast in the truth. Labor in my stead. If you survive, my death will be of little consequence." Luther looked steadily into his friend's face as he placed a load of writings into Melanchthon's hands. "Take these, publish them with the others, spread them all throughout Christendom. God's word shall not return void."

Embracing, Melanchthon reluctantly turned back toward the little village of Wittenberg.

"It is not too late to turn back, Martin. I fear the emperor will not honor your safe conduct." Spalatin's face was grave at the thought as they continued walking the lonely path.

Looking far beyond the hills down the road ahead of him, as if seeing beyond the present into the future ahead, Luther replied reticently, "God does not guide me, He pushes me forward. He carries me away. I am not master of myself. I desire to live in repose - but I am thrown into the midst of tumults and revolutions." His melancholy tone seemed strange coming from one so often viewed as an immovable stalwart of courage.

They walked in silence until they came to the outskirts of the village, each lost in thought of what surely lay ahead. As they passed through the gates of the small village they were greeted by the papal bull condemning Luther's writings to the flames posted on the gates.

"Our prayers and hearts go with you, my friend." His companion feared for Luther's courage and laid a reassuring hand on his shoulder. But fresh thoughts of the oppressive, tyrannical papal rule and the darkness of ignorance and superstition stupefying the common people roused the reformer's signature vehemence as he tore the bull off the posts and crushed it in his hands.

"Pray not for me, but for the word of God. Christ will give me His Spirit to overcome these ministers of error. I despise them during my life; I shall triumph over them by my death. They are busy at Worms about compelling me to retract; and this shall be my retraction: I said formerly that the pope was Christ's vicar; now I assert that he is our Lord's adversary, and the devil's apostle."

One of the mournful students accompanying him

regarded the bull woefully as he passed on behind them. "They will burn you, Professor Martin,"

Luther replied, "Though they should kindle a fire all the way from Worms to Wittenberg, the flames of which reached to heaven, I would walk through it in the name of the Lord. I will appear before them. I will enter the jaws of this behemoth, and break his teeth, confessing the Lord Jesus Christ." Turning from his friends, he stood resolutely staring down the road he must travel toward Worms.

He knew Satan was already at work, trying to tear down all that God was moving his servants to build up.

That evening, in another village not far away, an intrepid but humble peasant was smeared with pitch and tied to a stake. An angry cardinal in full regalia hissed into the poor man's face as he brandished a handful of Martin Luther's writings.

"Will you or will you not recant the doctrines of the heretic Luther?" The cardinal demanded.

"How can I deny my Lord?" The man quietly replied.

"Is Martin Luther indeed your lord?" The cardinal spat his angry retort. "Blasphemy!"

"Nay, but he has shown me that Jesus saith unto me, I am the way, the truth, and the life: no man cometh unto the Father, but by me." "You are an uneducated peasant! How dare you presume to teach me what the Scriptures say! You cannot understand them. We and the church fathers will tell you what they say and what they mean!" The cardinal was nearly unable to restrain himself as he shook in rage at what he perceived as the man's insurrection.

The man regarded him with piteous eyes as he answered meekly, appealing to what reason was left in his unreasonable accuser, "Jesus Himself said, suffer the little children to come unto me and forbid them not. If He calls even the children to Himself in His word, surely He made the Scriptures plain enough for even a child to understand."

Hardly listening as he paced in fury, the cardinal raged, "Repent of your blasphemous heretical babblings and beg me for forgiveness and absolution - or roast...for eternity!"

"My sins have gone before to my Holy Judge and Advocate, for Christ has said none can forgive but God alone."

"Heretic! This is blasphemy! Burn him! Burn him! Let not his foul breath taint the air we breathe with his fanatical ravings any longer!" Wild-eyed and outraged, the cardinal snatched the torch from the executioner's hand and tossed it onto the pile himself.

"Fear not them that can kill the body, but fear thou God alone," the pious man raised his eyes and voice to heaven as he cried from the thickening smoke, "Lord Jesus, into Thy hands I commend my spirit."

The horrified villagers, forced to witness the irrational interrogation and display of tyranny, drew back at the contrast of the two sides in the conflict as the cardinal's raging voice cut sharply through the hymn coming from the smoke and flames before him. "Heretic! Heretic! Burn him! Burn him! Burn! Burn! And cast his ashes into the Rhine! Burn them all! Let none of them have the right to speak before their execution lest they spread their heretical filth farther! Burn them!"

But the enemy of souls could not silence the faithful reformers. Said a Christian to the heathen rulers who were urging forward the persecution: "You may torment, afflict, and vex us. But your cruelty is of no avail. The more we are mowed down, the more we spring up again. The blood of the Christians is seed."

Stopping for a moment to rub his tired eyes, Gregory looked up from the large volume on the table in front of him. "How did he know he was right?"

Leaning back, he flipped through another nearby large volume. As he turned the pages, a large, folded insert flipped forward. Curiously, he pulled on it and it came out. He opened it out on the table, intrigued. It was a poster of a very old chart labeled "Martin Luther Time Prophecies from Daniel and Revelation". He tried to trace the time lines but could not make any sense of them.

Gregory was suddenly aware of how quiet and empty the library was as the custodian swept the floor beside him. Startled from his reverie, he looked up from the chart and checked his watch in surprise. Beside him, his laptop battery light was flashing. Clipping the lid shut, he slipped his computer into its case as he quickly gathered his things to leave. Tucking the poster back into the book, he tried to put it back on the high shelf and shoulder his computer at the same time, but he forgot to zip his bag shut and his computer nearly fell out. He dropped the large volume to catch his computer. The poster slipped out of the splayed pages of the sprawled book and slid under the shelf, unnoticed.

The rush of adrenalin left Gregory realizing just how thoroughly exhausted he was. He sighed as he pulled himself together. Slowly he zipped his computer case then picked up the book and shelved it. The library's eerie silence swallowed the hollow sound of his retreating steps as he hurried his weary feet toward the door.

Unseen, behind him, was another set of shoes, very nice shoes, that stepped forward to where Gregory had dropped the book. A hand felt under the shelf for the poster. Someone opened it briefly to see what Gregory was looking at, then tucked it into his jacket, turning to exit the library a different way.

Chapter 7

~ Practicing Bravery

Gregory had been sitting pensively at his desk for over an hour as Jeremy sprawled on his bed, studying quietly, listening to his mp3 player. Finally unnerved in the unusual stillness, Jeremy turned to face his friend, pulled his earphones out of his ears and leaned back on the cool dorm wall. It was abnormal to see Gregory sitting in silence staring at his blank computer screen.

"How is your thesis coming along?" Jeremy tentatively ventured.

Gregory swiveled back and forth a moment before he sighed deeply and answered, "I haven't started yet."

"Oh, that's not good." Jeremy swung his legs over the edge of the bed to get a better look at the blank page on Gregory's screen titled 'The Mark of the Beast'.

"What do *you* think the mark of the beast will be?" Gregory's usual enthusiasm was hindered by something Jeremy could not put his finger on.

"A barcode? Tattoo? A computer chip implant? Mind control?" Jeremy gently tried to coax Gregory's mood back to its normal, frolicking, carefree unpredictability. "I don't know. No one's going to know what is really going to happen until it happens, right? I mean, not even our professors know, and they're a lot smarter than we are. You picked a really hard topic. It's not too late to change it."

"I guess I'm all caught up in my mind with Melanie." Gregory blew his cheeks out as he ran his fingers through his messy hair.

"Oh, so she has a name?" Jeremy teased playfully.

"Who?" Gregory was still not himself.

"Your mysterious 'laundry girl'," Jeremy poked Gregory on the knee.

"Yeah, she's mysterious alright." Gregory's usual playful smile began to peek out the corners of his mouth as he swiveled back and forth in his chair at the thought of her. "I don't know how she got to know so much about the Bible and history, but every time we talk, she tells me to go study."

"Sounds about right." Jeremy smiled back, glad to see his friend's mood lighten. "Laundry girl knows more than Bible boy, - you never were top of your class... But you better get on your thesis or you'll be sticking around for another year..."

"Yeah. That'll be bad."

"Yeah. I'll miss you." Jeremy feigned a playful frown.

"Ha, ha, funny! You're going to miss me either way, we're both out of here this year!" Gregory tossed a magazine at his friend.

"Maybe...Can I ask you a serious question?" It was Jeremy who was now turning reticent.

"Maybe." Gregory hedged a smile, sensing his friend's rare vulnerability.

"Are you sure God wants you to be a pastor?" Jeremy hedged, avoiding eye contact.

Gregory considered a moment then answered resolutely, "Yes."

"How can you be so sure?" Jeremy pressed.

"You're not?" Feigning surprise, Gregory wondered how far he would be allowed to delve into his friend's mind.

"What if you love something else more?" Jeremy continued evading his probing eyes.

For a long moment, Gregory considered his answer carefully. Jeremy's eyes were riveted to the floor, so it was impossible to read them. Finally Gregory decided their friendship was strong enough to handle the answer forming on his lips. "Like...flying?"

Jeremy instantly retreated into himself as he babbled defensively, "Or... cooking or - I don't know, something!"

"Nah - it would have to be flying," Gregory tried to ease his friend's mind as he stretched his legs out and put his hands comfortably behind his head, smiling at Jeremy's distress, "No one can love cooking that much."

Jeremy looked away from Gregory's steady stare, feeling as though his life was written on the walls. Instinctively his eyes settled on his family picture, dominated by his smiling dad, his frail mom strapped to a wheelchair.

"Why don't you tell him?" Gregory hoped his tone sounded more sensitive than challenging.

"What?" The long suppressed bitterness spilled over unintentionally into Jeremy's tone, "That his only son wants to be a pilot instead of a preacher? That his 'mini-me' would rather go to the moon than be him?"

"Well, I don't think you should say it like that. Something more tactful would probably be more appropriate." Gregory shrugged trying to lighten the mood.

"He thinks the only reason that I have any interest in aeronautics is because I want to hide in the predictability of science rather than venture into the unpredictable realm of preaching about a God who can do everything, but doesn't choose to do anything." The familiar impasse played out in his mind as he relived the emotions from his earlier phone conversation with his dad.

"Is he right?" Gregory's tone was gentle, but urgent.

It took a long time for Jeremy to answer. "No. Maybe." He sighed. "...I don't know."

"I do." Gregory bravely smiled at his tortured friend.

"What? You think you're inside my head?" Jeremy didn't know whether to be relieved or offended at the thought that someone might actually understand him, or at least try to.

Gregory leaned forward, pressing his point home. "Jer, did you get a 4.0 in theology? Eschatology? Biblical exposition?"

"What have my grades got to do with this? They are private anyway." Jeremy hugged his pillow to his chest defensively.

"Sure. That is why they post them on the dorm bulletin board, right?" Gregory knocked him over with a gentle shove.

"Hey, I'm passing, that's all I need to do, right?" Jeremy caught himself, regaining his balance.

"How about Calculus? Physics I and II? You didn't miss a question - not even on the extra credit." Jeremy suppressed a proud smirk as Gregory recounted his triumphs. "Your brain's just wired differently. You read technical magazines from NASA and aeronautics engineering college text books for fun, for crying out loud! It's a talent! A passion! Not a crutch."

Jeremy's face showed that his heart was touched. "You really think so?"

Gregory pressed on gently, "Look, I have no idea what it feels like to have a mom with a painful, incurable disease." Jeremy looked away to hide his emotion. "But I do know that it takes real faith to keep believing that God is love in spite of watching her suffer, to keep trusting Him and in His greater plan for your lives, - to decide to believe that 'all things work together for good for those that love God and are called according to His purpose' - even though you don't understand the way He chooses to work things out."

Jeremy rubbed his eyes hard as he fought the flood of emotions threatening to well up again. Gregory studied at his friend's emotion-filled face carefully, then decided to continue, "Your faith isn't dead, Jer, even though you might feel like it is. Don't trust your feelings. Just trust God's word, like...like the instruments on the dash of the plane in a storm. You might feel you are flying upside-down, but they say you are right-side-up. If you go by feeling, you'll crash. You've got to go by the instrument, God's word."

Suddenly brightening, Jeremy smiled, red faced, "Hey, that's good! Where did you get that?"

"I read it in one of your flying magazines."

"Really? You knew all this time?" Relief flooded through Jeremy's face, threatening to release another powerful set of emotions.

"Well, no. Sort of. I think God just showed me recently, though it was there all the time," Gregory said as he looked away, allowing his friend time to regain control.

With a heaving sigh, Jeremy smiled and shrugged, unable to speak.

"Jeremy, I think you have a God-given talent, and I think you'll be miserable unless you are true to your calling. If your heart's not in what you do, what good is it anyway?"

Jeremy studied the picture over his bed, staring at his dad's beaming smile. "What about my dad?"

"He'll love you anyway. But you need to remember who your God is, who you follow, whose smile means the most to you."

"Ughhh, you're right. I know you're right." Jeremy tossed his pillow in the air and punched it to the bed, tension releasing from his body at every level from the relief of finally receiving affirmation.

Greg leaned over and punched his friend on the knee. Jeremy studied him as if for the first time. "You're going to make a really good pastor," Jeremy said seriously.

"Ya think?" Gregory crossed his eyes and stuck out his tongue.

"Yeah. I think." Jeremy shook his head, laughing.

"Thanks." Gregory smiled back, sincerely. The guy-closeness quickly felt awkward so Gregory broke it. "I'm hungry! Let's get out of here and find something to eat!" They laughed and Gregory stood to head out the door, Jeremy following behind him.

~

"Class, this is an example of the kind of work I am expecting for your thesis. This is a copy of Dr. James Gray's thesis on the rapture," Dr. Ribera's class received the paper he was handing to them with mixed emotions.

"Wasn't he one of the editors of the Scofield Bible?" an intrepid student ventured as he flipped through the pages.

"Good, you know your history." Dr. Ribera's terse lips almost gave in to a semblance of a smile as he stopped at Jeremy's desk. "And he's Jeremy great-grandfather, I understand. Or is it great-great-grandfather? I forget." Jeremy sank a little further down in his seat as the doctor shrugged at his obvious lack of enthusiasm at the compliment.

"Anyway, I thought you might like to know that the Scofield Society, a long standing sponsor of this Bible college, is going to be reviewing a random selection of your theses as part of their grant review to continue their funding of this school." A ripple of suppressed enthusiasm chorused through the class. "No pressure, just make sure that *all* your papers are worthy of that type of review. Make us proud of the type of pastors we are turning out of our doors. Make sure your theology is sound, - and Biblical." He gestured weakly as he added the last criteria, almost as an afterthought. "Show them you know what we teach here," he pondered a moment as if contemplating expounding on his list, but quickly lost the attention of the class as the buzzer sounds. "That's all folks, see you next week."

Jostling each other like cattle, the class filed out the door, inadvertently herding Gregory and Jeremy together.

"Wow, you're great-granddad's thesis. Pretty neat, huh?" Gregory was clearly animated at the thought as he held the papers in awe.

"Sure. Whatever." Jeremy shrugged as he unceremoniously dropped his copy into a nearby trashcan.

Oblivious, Gregory continued gushing, " 'No pressure' he says. I've *got* to get this discussion over with Melanie so I can concentrate on my thesis!"

"Yup. I'd say that's about right." Jeremy responded disinterestedly.

Gregory stopped in his tracks as an idea illuminated his countenance, "Hey - you got any laundry?"

Chapter 8

~ Opposition Strikes

Germany 1545
Concilium Tridentinum
The Council of Trent

A cardinal in ornate dress gazed with agitation out of the open window at large lighted bonfires below his parapet where several peasants and monks were being burned at the stake. His eyes glittered as he watched hooded henchmen toss books into the flames, fueling the already raging fires.

"It spreads like a plague, this Lutheran heresy." his stone faced expression and reticent tone suddenly exploded with the rage he could no longer suppress, "How dare he place the Holy Scriptures into the hands of the people!" His accompanying bishops exchanged a troubled glance as the sound of children crying and women screaming in the distance floated eerily on the dark night air in through the open window. Unaffected, he slipped into the ornate fur cape his paige was extending to him and took the hat from his outstretched hands. The lone, deep-throated monotonous chant of one of the monks perishing in the flames caused the young paige to turn from the window and shudder. "Jesus, Son of David, have mercy on me, have mercy on me." Over and over and over again the refrain repeated, a little fainter each time. Another of the men in the flames screamed uncontrollably. The Cardinal made no effort to conceal his distain as he regarded his paige's compassion as a weakness.

The bishops looked nervously at each other, "Yes, Your Grace, Martin Luther's heretical teaching and infernal writings are tearing the church apart." The skinny one ventured timidly.

"Fish mongers, smiths and weavers debate Holy Writ in our churches with *my* priests," the cardinal continued his rant as if not hearing any voice but his own.

"But the priests are not versed in the Scriptures, of course, only in the sayings of the church fathers...." The large bishop let his voice trail weakly, afraid to incur the cardinal's wrath by saying the wrong thing. He jumped nervously as the cardinal suddenly turned from the window again and began pacing slowly, with measured step, to the bowl of dried fruit the timid paige offered him. He picked up a date and scrutinized it.

"Luther must be stopped." He took a slow bite of the succulent date, then used it to gesture out of the window toward the martyrs suffering in the flames below him as he continued with measured words, "And this damage that *he* has done - must be corrected."

Another paige entered with his feathered cap under his arm. "Your Eminence, your horses are ready."

The cardinal finished his date and turned back to his window, paying no heed.

The timid, skinny bishop ventured with a mouse-like tone, "Must - must we travel to Trent... at night?"

As if in answer, the screams of the tortured below filtered again through the open window as a hail of stones pelleted the side of the castle, some of them making their way through the open window. The Cardinal stepped aside mildly to avoid his ornate robes being dirtied as he looked with deadly calm at the frail bishop. "Would you rather the peasants have the benefit of the light to their deadly aim? Or the blessed cover of the darkness to shelter us?"

Shamed, the fragile bishop bowed in respect, "Yes, of course, my lord."

"Let us all pray the decisions at the Council of Trent can stay this tide of evil... and save the mother church." The cardinal exited with a flourish as his paiges and bishops followed.

~

Gregory entered the laundromat anxiously toting two big bags of laundry, but Melanie was nowhere to be seen. He was visibly upset having walked there lugging the heavy bags. Then, just as he was about to leave she walked up behind him and ducked past to enter as he stood in the doorway, holding the door open.

"You must be a very messy guy to have generated so much laundry again in such a short time," she giggled.

"Oh, hey, I thought you weren't here," relief washed over his face.

"I have a late shift tonight, boss is on vacation, so I get to lock up."

"Great, so we can talk?"

Melanie laughed at his earnestness, "Why do I feel like one of those bags has a sleeping bag and pillow in it?"

"You know, that is a great idea. I wish I had thought of it!"

"Funny. I have to load a few machines, then I'll be free for a few minutes." Melanie shared another winning smile as she grabbed a few bags and started loading a machine.

"Yeah, me too," Gregory sighed and headed toward a machine.

A short while later, Gregory joined Melanie, sitting in the waiting chairs while their loads washed and Missy played quietly with the toys. "So, I've been reading up on the Reformation - amazing."

"Yes, but it's the Counter Reformation that holds the key to your 'beast' conundrum," Melanie flashed another of her special smiles.

"You keep saying that," Gregory answered, "I've told you just about everything I know. Now I'd like to hear what you have to say."

"Really? You might not like it," Melanie added a raised eyebrow to her whimsical smile.

"That's ok. I'd still like to hear it anyway."

"Ok, but remember you said that though!" She leaned forward thoughtfully waiting for the right starting place to come to mind as Gregory sat back patiently.

Unbeknownst to them, at that moment, the college president, James Todd, was clicking through the large list of thesis paper topics on his computer. He selected a few at random. Then, one in the list caught his eye. The topic read: "The Mark of the Beast, proposed by Gregory L. Martin". Intrigued, he scanned over the premise, shrugged, and then included it in the very small group he had selected to be sent to the Scofield Society. He began his email, speaking out loud as he typed, "Dear Sirs, attached is a list of thesis topics. You will be receiving shortly a copy of the drafts of these papers by mail for your review as a random sample of one of our classes..." He finished typing and attached the list of topic papers, then sent the email just as Gregory and Melanie were finishing their study...

Gregory's face and posture communicated his mixed emotions. "Wow. That's a lot to think about."

"I know. I know how you feel. Just study it out a while, and pray."

"I will be. This changes a lot." He sat back and rubbed his face wearily. "Hey, how did you get to know so much about the Bible?"

"I'm a PK." Melanie shrugged.

Gregory smiled incredulously. "You? A preacher's kid? I'd never have guessed." He inadvertently glanced at her tattoos.

"Yeah, well, a famous missionary once very rightly noted that 'a mouse born in a cookie jar is not a cookie'." Melanie answered defensively, "Just because my dad was a preacher, doesn't mean his kids are automatically born saved."

Gregory didn't mean to offend his sensitive new friend as he replied gently, "Actually, I think the opposite is true."

"What?" Melanie was disarmed.

"I think the devil works extra hard on the families of those who work the hardest for God. If he can hurt the family, he might be able to stop the zeal of the most dedicated."

"Yeah, well, not everyone sees it that way, and I know I've caused my family, especially my dad, a lot of pain."

"How long has it been since you saw him?"

Melanie sighed softly, "Before Missy was born. I ran away when I found out I was pregnant. It's crazy how things turned out. I had just hit rock bottom and given my heart to God, for real this time, and then... well, I just couldn't stand to cause my dad any more pain. So I left."

"What!? So he - he never knew? About you, about your conversion, about Missy?"

"He was going through so much. I just couldn't add to it. I was a baby Christian - I thought leaving was the right thing to do. I'd do it differently if I had to do it all over again. I really miss him. You know he was a graduate from Martin Luther Bible College."

"No, I didn't know that. I should look him up, what was his name?" Gregory's interest was piqued.

"Stanley Wilkinson. His picture was in the hall of faith. Funny isn't it? That I should end up back here. I often ask God why." She studied Gregory's expression, and she wondered how much he knew.

Later that night, Greg sat typing at his laptop in earnest, a pencil in his mouth, surrounded by books. His thesis was taking shape as he attached his initial draft as an email to Dr. Ribera.

~

The next day, the president's secretary, Judy, had just finished printing the draft thesis papers to send for board review, but was missing Gregory's from the list. Her watch showed it was nearly lunch and she wanted to drop off the package on her lunch break. At this rate, she knew she was going to be late. She quickly scanned through the emails sent to Dr. Ribera. Finally Gregory's topic, "The Mark of the Beast," caught her eye in the long list on her screen. Smiling triumphantly, she printed it out and checked his name, the last one missing, off of the list that James Todd had left for her. She gathered the other papers she had already printed, placed Gregory's on top, and put the president's form letter on top of the entire stack. Quickly she stamped it with his signature, and sealed the envelope. There was a calendar based list on the white board beside her that had "mail out thesis prelims for board review" written in bold, red capital letters. She crossed it off the list, and then gathered the remaining mail from the "out" box, grabbed her purse and keys, and left for the post office, flipping her "in" sign beside her name on the board to "out" on her way through the door.

~

Back in the dorm room, an adamant Jeremy tossed Gregory's thesis draft on the bed.

"You can't turn that in. It's too controversial." Jeremy hoped the firm tone in his voice would sway his enthusiastic friend.

"It's the truth. The truth is *always* controversial."

"How do you know it's true?" Jeremy retorted, "Just because some girl you just met says so?"

"No, because I've studied it out." Gregory smiled a big beaver grin, pointing to his growing pile of library books and his well thumbed Bible on top.

Jeremy flailed his arms in exasperation, "If you turn that in, they'll fail you."

"How do you know that? Besides, I already emailed in my first revision for review."

"You turned that in!?" Jeremy's exasperation escalated to near panic at the thought.

"Maybe this is the beginning of a revival of the old paths - you know, the Martin Luther Bible College getting back to its roots." Gregory sat down at his desk and spun around in his chair slowly. "Someone's got to lead the way."

"And it's not you." Jeremy looked at his oblivious friend firmly. "Look, I gotta go. Just don't get me involved, ok? You still have enough time to write a new thesis. Just talk to Dr. Ribera and tell him you need more time." He swung his backpack on his shoulder and grabbed his coat.

"Dr. Ribera, huh?" Gregory grinned.

"Oh, come on. It's just a coincidence." Jeremy threw his hands up defeated and left.

Chapter 9

~ Fiery Trials

A few days later, the president was sitting at his desk working on some paperwork when Judy opened the door nervously and peeked her head in. "Sir, urgent call for you on line two."

Looking up from his papers James Todd smiled and answered the phone cheerily, "James Todd. Well, hello, Pastor Irving, did you receive the thesis drafts we sent you?" His expression changed as the color drained out of his face. "...Oh dear." Judy cringed as she heard yelling faintly coming from the person on the other line.

Soon after, the president himself was very red-faced, pacing and flailing Gregory's thesis in his

hand, while screaming at the dean and Dr. Ribera who were sitting in his office.
"This pipsqueak of a student's thesis is threatening to disqualify us for the grant. Make him change it! Now!"

~

1545 A.D.

Ornately dressed pontiffs, bishops, cardinals, and finally the pope seated themselves pretentiously in the council hall with much pomp and ceremony. A dog-faced man with a scroll walked to the center of the hall and spoke loudly in his monotone voice.

"This Council at Trent in the year of our Lord 1545 is now convened by order of his holiness Pope Paul III for the purpose of destroying the heresy purported by the heretic, Martin Luther, and his adherents and restoring the order and supremacy of the Holy Roman Catholic church. Amen." The bailiff tapped his staff loudly on the marble floor.

~

Gregory shuffled his feet nervously and turned the page in the book he was reading as he sat uneasily outside of Dr. Ribera's class. Another student exited, holding his paper in his hands and morosely studying the multitudinous red revision notes smattering the pages in the doctor's fluid handwriting. Greg stood as the other student passed by. He entered the class nervously. Dr. Ribera was seated at his desk alone with mounds of papers surrounding him. Greg's thesis was in front of him. He noticed his name and topic were circled in red.

Dr. Ribera motioned for him to sit. Taking a deep breath Greg sat down and waited expectantly for the Dr. to speak first. He paused, measuring his words, then began.

"Gregory, I understand you have put a considerable amount of time and effort into your draft thesis," the doctor looked at Gregory kindly as he meticulously interlaced his fingers firmly.

"Yes, sir," Gregory shifted uneasily in his seat.

"So, it is with regret that I must urge you to change your thesis topic." The doctor began writing on the next student's paper, indicating that the discussion was over. Gregory looked confused a moment.

"What? I don't understand. I don't want to choose a different topic -" he hoped his tone was more respectful than it sounded as he tried to reign in his assertiveness. He need not have worried, as the doctor continued writing as if he had not heard.

"I have already cleared your extension with the department heads. We are all standing behind you, ready to help you. Just choose a different topic." He punctuated his last sentence with a steady stare.

"But what about my paper, my research? What did you think about what I wrote?"

Dr. Ribera's stern tone and manner ended the interview. "I will expect your new topic by Friday. Do I make myself clear?"

~

Back in his dorm room, a frustrated Gregory threw himself into his chair, upset. He threw his book bag on the floor angrily, and sat spinning in the chair, looking up at the ceiling. Jeremy looked at him from over an aeronautics magazine.

"I hate to say I told you so."

Gregory didn't acknowledge him.

"I think we both know what you have to do..." Jeremy turned the page slowly.

"Yes." Gregory spun himself around again as he sighed heavily. Jeremy looked relieved as Gregory stood up resolutely and began gathering his papers. "I have to go see the dean. He'll understand - all I need is a chance to explain."

Jeremy shook his head in disbelief as Gregory passed him and disappeared down the hall.

~

James Todd's already red face color deepened as he paced, flipping through the thesis in his hand. His secretary poked her head in the door timidly.

"Professor Schwarzerd is -"

"Send him in." He interrupted angrily.

The professor entered calmly, taking in the storm in the room.

"This better not be something you started, Gerhard, I don't need to remind you that you haven't made tenure, do I?" He shoved a copy of Gregory's thesis into the professor's hands.

Professor Schwarzerd looked back at him with obvious concern, then glanced over a few of the pages as his eyebrows raised in surprise. Sensing the president didn't call him to discuss the matter, he nodded respectfully, pondering his response carefully as he handed the papers back to James Todd. "Thank you for the reminder, sir," he paused thoughtfully, then added, "If God is for us who can be against us? If this counsel, or this work be of men, it will come to nought: But if it be of God, ye cannot overthrow it; lest haply ye be found even to fight against God." James Todd stared hard at him as he turned to leave quietly.

The professor passed by Gregory in the hall and nodded an acknowledgement quietly as Gregory walked purposefully down the hall of faith and knocked on the door. Pausing thoughtfully a moment, he began looking at each of the names under each picture for Stanley Wilkinson's name. He got to the spot where there was a name and photo missing and quickly checked the photos after, but did not find him. He went back to the empty spot and studied the place where the name plate was. "Stanley Wilkinson" could be faintly seen scratched out. Gregory's face registered his curiosity and interest.

Behind him, the dean opened his door across from the president's office and motioned for Greg to come in. He eased into a seat in the dean's office as the dean seated himself slowly at his desk. He instinctively felt that he should not speak first. His heart raced as he suppressed his words and waited anxiously for the dean to start.

The dean studied Gregory for a moment, then opened a file on his desk and flipped slowly through the pages. Finally he looked up at Gregory again, who was still waiting and a little on edge.

"Greg, you have a clean file, good grades, your teachers like you," Greg gratefully acknowledged the compliments and let himself ease back into the chair. "Why do you want to end that?"

Gregory squirmed defensively, caught off guard, "I - I don't, Dean, but I should be able to say what I believe, right?"

"You're in school, at a Bible college. The students that come from a school are supposed to represent and embody the teachings of the school they graduate from." The dean leveled a firm stare at Gregory.

"Sir, with all due respect, I feel like you are more worried about getting money for the school than teaching truth," Gregory tried to keep his voice under control.

"Do you think it's wrong for alumni to support their alma maters?" Gregory's brow furrowed at the dean's subtle attack. "This school has been supported by grants since its founding. Why do you feel it best to have the school close?" "Dean, I'm not trying to close the school - I'm at the Martin Luther Bible College, and I am merely writing my thesis on what Martin Luther believed." The dean feigned a sigh of relief and laughed, "Is *that* what you think you are doing?"

"Yes," Gregory asked, puzzled, "why, what do you think I am doing?"

"Well," Dean Bellarmine chuckled to himself, then paused, studying Gregory slyly, "I noticed that you have had an unusual amount of laundry lately."

Gregory squirmed uneasily under the dean's probing stare. "Laundry, sir?"

"I was wondering if you might not be letting yourself be carried away with the fanciful ideas of a young and pretty girl who might be putting a little... undue influence on you." Dean Bellarmine leaned toward Gregory, searching his face as he spoke slowly, "...by using her feminine charms, maybe?" Gregory looked surprised. He had no idea the dean even knew about Melanie. "I'm sure you know that Melanie Wilkinson, well, shall we say, has an ax to grind - because of what happened to her father."

"Stanley Wilkinson?" Gregory tried to hedge his curiosity, "What happened to him?"

"Oh, terrible scandal," Dean Bellarmine leaned back into his chair as he savored his words deliciously. "He brought so much...pain...to the college when he told us about his daughter's indiscretions. Pastor's daughter...teenage pregnancy, - well, if you can't rule your own house, how can you lead a church? We had no choice but to remove him from the hall of faith and publicly revoke his Doctor of Theology."

"Really?" Gregory could not hide his surprise, "Is *that* what happened?"

"She may have told you differently - loyal, but misguided. You see what a high standard we hold our graduates to, Mr. Gregory - before *and* after they graduate. Our students must show that they embody our beliefs," he leaned forward again intensely, "all of them. Do you understand?" Gregory nodded mechanically. "Good. I'll let Dr. Ribera know he should be expecting your new topic by the end of the week." He closed the file on his desk and smiled as Gregory stood to leave. "And, Mr. Gregory, if I could offer you a bit of advice," Greg turned to face him at the door. "Stay away from Melanie Wilkinson. You know the college's policy on dating. And she already has... a reputation, if you understand what I mean." Greg nodded again and left wordlessly.

Gregory sighed heavily as he slipped back into the dorm room. Jeremy was still lying on his bed reading and didn't look up when Greg entered.

"I hate when I can say 'I told you so.' I really hate it." He turned a page quietly. Gregory sat in his chair and puffed out his cheeks in a large exhale.

"Me too."

Jeremy eyed his friend over the top of his magazine. "I hope you aren't coming to me for advice. I really don't know what you should do."
"Me neither."

Hours later, Jeremy was sleeping in his bed with the pillow over his head and Gregory was still sitting pensively at his desk reflecting in silent grief and agitation. Finally, lying down on his bed, fully dressed, on top of the covers, he stared at the ceiling. All too soon, faint beams of sunlight started filtering through the blind as the sun began to rise. Jeremy woke and stretched, then stumbled, disheveled, toward the bathroom with his tooth brush and towel. Gregory, now alone and still wide awake, rolled out of bed onto his knees and prayed.

He was still on his knees when Jeremy slipped back in, dressed and tidy. He looked silently at his friend in prayer, quietly grabbed his book bag and jacket and slipped out, closing the door after him gently.

"Lord, show me what to do. Show me what is right." He grabbed his Bible and it fell open to highlighted verses in 1 Peter 4:12, 13. He read aloud, "Beloved, think it not strange concerning the fiery trial which is to try you, as though some strange thing happened unto you: But rejoice, inasmuch as ye are partakers of Christ's sufferings; that, when his glory shall be revealed, ye may be glad also with exceeding joy." Staring at the verse a moment, he picked up his pen and paper and began writing while still on his knees.

Chapter 10

~ The Battle Begins

In the library, the mysterious person who had picked up the time chart was seated in one of the plush emperor style chairs by the window, slowly turning the pages of an ancient leather bound book, stopping at an artist's depiction of the council of Trent, in full swing.

"Your time has expired. You are required to make your decision. Will you adhere to your absurd declaration of 'Scripture alone'? Or agree with your mother church that truth is determined upon Scripture *and* tradition?" The orator's face reddened as he demanded an answer.

The reformers looked despairingly at each other, then their pale and haggard spokesperson stood and spoke haltingly. "Archbishop Reggio, Venerable Council, we humbly ask you to point out to us wherein we have erred."

"You must revoke all your errors, and embrace the true doctrine of the Church." The Archbishop Reggio's veins stood out on his temple as he suppressed his rage and spat out the words contemptuously.

Again the humble speaker ventured, "We ask for Scripture; it is on Scripture that our views are founded."

"Do you not know that the Pope is above all?" The archbishop replied haughtily.

"Not above Scripture." The reformer's voice, though tired, rang loud and clear through the hall.

Unable to contain himself the archbishop raged, "Yes, above Scripture, and above councils. Retract, retract!"

~

Gregory looked both ways down the deserted sidewalk, then opened the laundromat door and entered furtively, looking for Melanie. He saw her folding a large pile of laundry at a table. He tucked his hands deep into his pockets and made his way quickly toward her, head bowed as he scanned the corners of the room. It was empty. She smiled when she saw him and Missy waved from under the table shyly.

"Hands down, you are the messiest guy I know!" Her sparkling smile danced on her lips.

Gregory smiled at the jibe. "Hi."

She looked at his empty hands, puzzled. "Where is your laundry bag?"

"I didn't come to do laundry...I..." Gregory shifted from one foot to another as he look around the room, avoiding her inquiring eyes, "I came to say...goodbye." Melanie stopped folding and looked at him critically. "I really appreciate everything that you've shared with me."

She let her jaw drop as she searched for words, then pursed her lips together and put her hand on her hip. "Let me guess, they didn't like your paper." Gregory studied his shoes. "Well, if you can't take the heat, then get out of the kitchen, right?" She began folding again energetically.

"Look, it's not like that," Gregory looked at her in dismay. She ignored him and continued folding furiously. Annoyed he blurted, "I mean, this is my life, my life work. I really believe this is what God has called me to do with my life - to be a pastor. Don't you understand what that means?"

Melanie stopped folding and put her hand on her hip again. "Sure. I know exactly what that means. It means that some paper from some college, or some denominational endorsement is more important to you than the truth."

"Is it the truth?" Gregory probed.

Melanie looked at him in exasperation. "You are the one who studied it out, you tell me." Gregory studied his shoes again. "You think you're fooling God? You think He doesn't know when we sell out? He gave you a brain and He gave you information and He asks you to learn and study for yourself. 'Study to show thyself approved' - to who? The dean? Don't you see how important this is?" He still won't meet her earnest gaze. She softened, seeing his distress. "Look, I know it's hard. I know it's a struggle. But you're not the first person to be in this situation, and you're for sure not going to be the last. Following God takes bravery and courage. Being true to your convictions, no matter what, takes courage and real faith. Hearing God for *yourself* instead of listening to what everyone says is critical to salvation. Don't you understand that?"

"Is it really that big of a deal?" Gregory shrugged, looking out the window.

"Gregory, you're not just sweeping a small point of truth under the rug, it's a huge thing. If more of God's people would stand up and be brave about what He has revealed, a lot of people would not fail when the final test comes!"

Suddenly annoyed, Gregory's face hardened. "Look, I've got to leave. I'm sorry." Realizing his annoyance is more at himself than Melanie he caught himself and softened. "I'm really glad I met you though, and I'll be praying for you."

"Fine. Have a nice cushy life of constant compromise and people pleasing." Melanie tossed another badly folded shirt on the pile she was working on.

"Hey! That's a little rough, don't you think? You have no idea what I am going through here!"

"Don't I?" She threw the shirt she was folding down in a crumpled heap, "How do you think I know so much about this stuff? My dad preached it - all over the place, it's drilled into my head! The churches couldn't get enough of the truth, he couldn't keep up with the invitations. People started asking questions - important questions - questions that change things. And change is never easy. Why do you think they stripped him of his credentials? They tried to destroy him!" she turned passionately toward Gregory with red-rimmed eyes.

Gregory turned away defensively, "That's not what they said! They said it was you - because of Missy -" He caught himself, but it was too late. Melanie recoiled, visibly hurt.

"What?!"

"I'm sorry," his regretful tone couldn't take the words back though.

"And you believed them?! I told you my dad doesn't even know about Missy! - you know what? You're just like them. They deserve you. Go graduate, ok?" She turned away from him, unable to check her angry tears as he stood there, awkwardly watching her.

"Look, I'm sorry. I don't know what to believe any more."

Melanie stared at him earnestly with red-rimmed eyes, "Believe God's Word."

After an awkward silence he glanced at the door again as someone came in to check their load. "I have to go. I didn't mean to hurt you." She ignored him as she stopped to blow her nose, then resumed folding.

"Bye." He watched her a while, not knowing what to say. She continued to ignore him, so he turned to go. Giving one last look over his shoulder he saw Missy staring at him sadly from under the table. She waved a sad, slow little wave with her mouth turned down in a frown that wasn't meant to be cute, but could not be otherwise on her pretty little face. He nodded sadly and stepped out the door, letting it swing shut behind him.

As soon as he was gone, Melanie stopped folding the large pile of laundry in front of her as she bowed her head and let the sobs wrack her frame for a moment. Missy sadly began playing with blocks under the table as the dean stood outside the laundromat, watching them, unnoticed, through the dirty windows. Satisfied, he tucked his hands deep in his pockets, then walked slowly down the side walk.

A few hours later, Gregory wordlessly entered Dr. Ribera's class with the other students in his class. Walking up to Dr. Ribera's desk, he handed a page of his notes to him silently.

"Ah, your new thesis topic?" Dr. Ribera scanned the paper quickly. "First Peter 4. Very nice. I look forward to reading it. Thank you," he dropped the page on top of the pile on his desk tersely and continued writing as Gregory walked silently to his seat and sat down, defeated.

~

That evening, Gregory sat at a desk in the library with his laptop open, staring into space. A shadowy figure silently came up behind him holding a stack of bound manuscripts and sat down, unnoticed, placing them quietly on the table.

"Do you know what happens to all the thesis papers the students write?" The voice from behind him startled Gregory out of his reverie.

"No, I don't," He turned to face the voice and was surprised to see Fitz sitting across the table from him.

"They file them in the vault section of the library." Gregory didn't see a connection, or care in light of the turmoil in his life. Still, he managed to smile and nod politely. Unfazed, Fitz continued deliberately, opening one of the manuscripts. "I've been reading them." He flattened out a marked page and read out loud, "We have nothing to fear for the future - except as we forget how God has lead us in the past." He looked up at Gregory with his penetrating blue eyes. "Poignant point, don't you think?" He picked up one of the books Greg was reading about the Reformation. "When you were reading these books, didn't you ever wonder what gave Martin Luther and the other reformers the courage to finally stand for the truths in God's word, no matter what the cost?"

Gregory looked questioningly at Fitz, then slowly shook his head, his interest piqued. He listened quietly as Fitz continued. "Everything Luther was preaching - the free forgiveness offered by Jesus, His saving love, the character of God - all went directly against the popular teachings of the church, which were steeped in paganism and devil worship, having no Bible to reveal the truth to them. You can imagine what a battle it was for him to be constantly at odds theologically with the church he loved so much. He truly believed his leaders were just delusional, misinformed, and was sure that if they could know the Word of God as he did, they would be reconciled."

"Is it so wrong to want to have peace?" Gregory looked down at the decorative carvings and inlays on the ornate library desk.

"Only if peace comes at the expense of truth." Fitz's eyes were unflinching as Gregory stole a look in his direction.

"I don't want to start a war." Gregory sighed and ran his fingers through his messy hair. "They say I am trying to destroy the school."

Fitz shrugged. "Martin Luther was accused of trying to destroy the church. This caused him much perplexity and distress." He watched Gregory tracing the patterned inlay on the desk. "You know, he couldn't break free of his doubts until the Lord opened his understanding of the prophecies of Daniel and Revelation."

"Why are you helping me?" Gregory tried vainly to probe the depths of those steel blue eyes.

Fitz spread the chart Gregory had dropped on the library floor onto the table.

"Hey - I saw this the other night, but I couldn't make any sense of it. What is it?"

"It's a map - through time - and if you follow it, you'll find what you are looking for." Fitz leveled his gaze at Gregory. "Do you have your Bible handy?"

"Sure," Gregory pulled his worn copy from his book bag as Fitz began tracing the lines on the page as he smoothed it out.

"Here, see this line? It's the 49 weeks from Daniel 9:25."

"Yeah, I recognized that part, but the rest is really different. I mean, what are the beasts from Revelation doing here?"

"Well, it might surprise you to know that this is the original, and I believe, *correct* understanding of the time prophecies. The new understanding they are teaching here did not come until later."

Gregory's brow furrowed suspiciously, "Why are you telling me this?"

"Because those thesis papers I was reading in the vault from three generations ago used to teach what's on this chart too." Fitz watched Gregory's face register a gamut of emotions.

"Really?" He looked incredulously at Fitz.

"Over time, the curriculum changed - around the 1900's - when they adopted the Scofield Bible..."

Gregory's eyes widened as he interrupted, "- the grant that keeps the school open is from the Scofield Bible Society! But why is it so important that all the students from Martin Luther Bible College agree with them? Why not just find a new sponsor?"

"Good question." Fitz stood and swung his bag over his shoulder as he stood to leave. "I guess you have a lot to think about."

For a moment Gregory watched Fitz disappear down the corridor as he stared at the chart, then quickly packed up his things, grabbing the chart, and started jogging back toward his room.

He quickly sat at his desk, staring at a partially typed page on his laptop, twirling his pencil, and swaying back and forth in his chair. His eyebrows twitched in thought as a verse popped in his head. Grabbing his Bible, he flipped through the pages to a highlighted verse in Proverbs 11:14 "Where no counsel is, the people fall: but in the multitude of counselors there is safety." He looked up at Jeremy, who was sitting on his bed, studying as his head bobbed to the music on his mp3 player.

He flipped back a few pages to Deuteronomy 19:15 "One witness shall not rise up against a man for any iniquity, or for any sin, in any sin that he sinneth: at the mouth of two witnesses, or at the mouth of three witnesses, shall the matter be established."

He let the words sink in as he stared at the pages a moment as a plan formulated in his mind, then, sitting a little straighter, he turned back to his computer, pencil in his mouth, and began typing with renewed enthusiasm, looking at his Bible and flipping frequently through its pages, Gregory worked long into the night.

Chapter 11

~ Faint Light Begins to Dawn

Early the next morning, Gregory leaned back on his chair, bleary-eyed, rubbing his shoulders and stretching as he yawned while his printer worked. He picked up the large stack of papers that just finished printing off the printer. Putting a bulldog clip on them, he laid them on his bed as he knelt beside them and prayed out loud softly.

"Lord, please, please show me what you want me to do... And then give me the courage to do it. Amen." A voice at the open door startled him.

"I guess you've been taking some heat," Fitz said quietly as he appeared in his doorway, his laptop and Bible under his arm.

"We're told the fire is not to consume, but refine, right?" Greg stood in respect when he saw him. "Good to see you again, Fitz. Want to sit down?" He cleared his messy clothes off the other chair, tossing them onto his bed, and gestured toward the seat. Fitz eased into the chair.

"I just really felt like I should show you something I've been working on. Do you mind?" Fitz lifted his laptop to desk height, but the desk was covered with papers and empty cups, cans and pizza plates.

"Sure, sure!" With one swipe of his arm, Gregory bulldozed the litter off the edge of the desk, some of it landing in the trash, most missing. Fitz put his laptop down and pulled out a large capacity jump drive. Plugging it in, he opened the lid, and a graphic came to life on the screen. "Nice laptop - serious!"

"Yeah, my dad owns a big animation firm. He let me come to seminary, but he didn't want me to quit animation, so he hooked me up. He pulls me out of class when he needs me. I guess big shot alumni can do that." Fitz grinned.

"Really? We always wondered where you went."

Jeremy came into the room holding a candy bar and soda, astonished to see Fitz. They were never more than acquaintances.

"Oh, hey, Fitz - nice computer."

"Thanks, come on over, I think you want to see this too." Jeremy seated himself on the end of his bed and watched the screen as a series of animations began to illustrate Fitz's explanation.

Fitz pointed to a section of the timeline on his screen. "These 7 years are the current focus of the left behind theory - their starting date is kind of hanging in space, waiting for the secret rapture to indicate they have started... But check this out. What if we leave them intact - attached to the 490 years in Daniel 2. It then pinpoints the crucifixion - accurately."

"Years? It says days." Jeremy said with his mouth full.

"Yes, a day stands for a year in Bible prophecy Remember how the Israelites had to wander in the desert 40 years, a year for each day the spies searched the land?" Fitz answered.

"I keep forgetting. There's other places for that too, right?" Jeremy opened his second candy bar.

"Yeah, a lot of places." Gregory grinned at him. Jeremy shrugged and took a bite of his candy bar as Fitz brought up another graphic.

"Check this out. Daniel 9:24: '70 weeks are determined upon thy people...' That Hebrew word 'determined' means 'cut off'. What were the 490 years 'cut off' of?"

Jeremy shrugged, "I don't know."

"The only time prophecy mentioned before this is the 2300 days in Daniel 8. Daniel was asking the

Lord, 'how long' - how long till the promises of God are fulfilled? He was talking about the restoration of Jerusalem, but God revealed much more than that. Look at this - " Fitz gestured toward the timeline animation unfolding on his screen as he held his open Bible on his lap. "Here are the 7 years, intact with the 490, intact with the 2300 days. 'From the going forth of the commandment to restore and to build Jerusalem unto the Messiah the Prince shall be seven weeks, and threescore and two weeks' - namely, sixty-nine weeks, or 483 years. The decree of Artaxerxes went into effect in the autumn of 457 B.C. From this date, 483 years extend to the autumn of A.D. 27. At that time, this prophecy was fulfilled."

"How?" Jeremy sat down on the edge of his bed to see the screen better.

"The Hebrew word 'Messiah' means 'the Anointed One'. In the autumn of A.D. 27, Jesus, the Messiah, was baptized by John and received the anointing of the Spirit. John 'saw the Spirit descending from heaven like a dove, and it abode upon him.' John 1:32. The Scriptures tell us in Acts 10:38 that 'God anointed Jesus of Nazareth with the Holy Ghost and with power.' And the Saviour Himself declared: 'The Spirit of the Lord is upon Me, because He hath anointed Me to preach the gospel to the poor.' Luke 4:18. After His baptism He went into Galilee, 'preaching the gospel of the kingdom of God, and saying, The time is fulfilled'."

Gregory's face lit up, "He meant the *time* prophecy in Daniel was fulfilled! Incredible."

"There's more - check this out - and it fits perfectly with the 7 years we were talking about earlier." Fitz flipped through his Bible eagerly and read, "'And He shall confirm the covenant with many for one week.' Now, keeping things in chronological order, this would then be the last seven years of the 490 year period allotted especially to the Jews. Remember the angel said it was 'cut off' of the 2300 'for thy people' - Daniel's people were the literal Jews. During this time, extending from A.D. 27 to A.D. 34, Christ, at first in person and afterward by His disciples, extended the gospel invitation especially to the Jews. The Saviour's direction was: 'Go not into the way of the Gentiles, and into any city of the Samaritans enter ye not: but go rather to the lost sheep of the house of Israel.' Matthew 10:5, 6."

Gregory interrupted, "Wait, but the prophecy said that 'in the midst of the week He shall cause the sacrifice and the oblation to cease.' What does that mean chronologically?"

"In A.D. 31, exactly three and a half years after His baptism, Jesus was crucified, ending the system of offerings which for four thousand years had pointed forward to the coming of Lamb of God. Type met antitype, and all the sacrifices and oblations of the ceremonial system were to cease. Remember the veil in the temple was torn from top to bottom when Jesus died on the cross? That was God sending a message that the old system of coming to Him through a priest and a sacrificed lamb was over – Jesus opened the way for us to come to the Father directly through Him, our heavenly High Priest and perfect sacrifice forever."

"Amazing. It fits together like a puzzle." Gregory said as he studied the graphic on the screen.

"At the end of the 7 years, in A.D. 34, through the action of the Jewish Sanhedrin, the Jewish nation sealed its rejection of being the special carriers of the gospel by the martyrdom of Stephen and by the persecution of the followers of Christ. Then the message of salvation was no longer restricted to the literal Jews, and went out to the world. The disciples, forced by persecution to flee from Jerusalem, 'went everywhere preaching the word'."

Gregory nodded, "That's right, Philip went down to the city of Samaria, Peter, opened the gospel to Cornelius, the gentile centurion of Caesarea, and Paul was commissioned by God to carry the glad tidings 'far hence unto the Gentiles'."

"Yes, Biblically, from that point, all who accept the gospel become sons and daughters of God, spiritual Israel. This was a critical turning point in the identity of the nation. They were no longer to point forward to a coming Messiah – through the sacrifice of lambs, but backward, to a risen Messiah – through the spreading of the Gospel of the risen Christ. Before the cross, those who embraced the Gospel message of a coming Messiah became literal Jews and embraced the sacrifice of lambs which pointed to the coming Lamb of God. Now those types and ceremonies had been fulfilled, and when a person becomes a child of God, they accept Jesus' sacrifice on their behalf and become a member of spiritual Israel – overcomers in the blood of the Lamb." Fitz clicked a few times and brought up another graphic.

"Amazing. The 7 years is part of the 490 years, which is part of the 2300." Gregory pointed to the connected sections on the time line.

"That's right. It's all one prophecy," Fitz zoomed out to show the entire line. "The early reformers believed that all the time prophecies in Daniel and Revelation - the 490 years, the 70 weeks, the 2300 days, - all of them, were intertwined and connected, and were essentially talking about the same time period." Fitz's graphic of the connected timelines illuminated his screen.

"What? What is the point of that?" Gregory asked.

"It's like having three dimensional coordinates to pinpoint a spot in space." Fitz answered, pushing his glasses up as they slid down his nose.

"That makes sense, the more points you have to confirm the spot, the more sure you can be that you have the right spot. It's called 'triangulating'." Jeremy took a big bite of his candy bar.

"So, where does the 2300 days end?" Jeremy asked, opening his third candy bar.

"1844." Fitz answered as he continued typing.

"And...What happened in 1844?" Jeremy was about to take a bite of his bar when Gregory grabbed it.

"You shouldn't eat too many of these, you know," Greg said as he stuffed it in his mouth. Jeremy shot an irked look at his friend as he took another out of his pocket and opened it in defiance, taking a big bite.

"I'll get to that in a sec - just check this out first," he brought up another animation file. "It's another time prophecy in Daniel - called the 1260 - you find it in Daniel 7. You'll like this a lot, check it out. Here is the beast with the 10 horns, the 10 divisions of Europe that came up after the Roman Empire fell. Three are plucked up from the roots - destroyed - the Vandals, Ostrogoths, Huruli."

"Vandals? Is that where we get the word 'vandalism'?" Jeremy asked, amused.

"Actually, yes," Fitz answered studiously. "The Vandals wanted a purer religion, free from idolatry, so they smashed the statues of Isis, Horus, Jupiter and Saturn that were being brought into the churches under new names, like Mary, Jesus, Paul and Peter."

"So, they were the good guys, and now we think of them as the bad guys." Jeremy finished his candy bar and tossed the wrapper toward the overflowing trashcan – and missed.

"Vandalism in the name of the Lord?" Gregory quipped.

"Look at this," Fitz gestured toward his illustration, "Daniel 7:24, 25 says 'the ten horns out of this kingdom are ten kings that shall arise: and another shall rise after them; and he shall be diverse from the first - different because it is not merely a political power, but a hybrid of a political-religio power. 'And he shall subdue three kings. And he shall speak great words against the most High, and shall wear out the saints of the most High, and think to change times and laws: and they shall be given into his hand until a time and times and the dividing of time'."

"Times? What kind of time prophecy is that? There's no numbers, no days." Gregory asked.

"Always use the Bible to explain its own language." Fitz flipped through his Bible again to Daniel chapter four, "When Nebuchadnezzar fell because of pride, God said the king was to be like a beast in the field until 7 'times' pass over him. Seven years later, the king came to his senses."

"Ok, so, a time - one year, times... at least 2 years, and the dividing of a time - half a year?" Gregory jotted down the numbers on his notepad. "So, three and a half years, corresponding with the same prophecy in Revelation 12 where the woman, God's true church, was hidden in the wilderness and sustained by God for the exact same time period." He grabbed his calculator and began adding.

Jeremy blinked and auto-calculated in his head. "That's three and a half years, 360 years to a Hebrew year - so 360 times three, plus half of 360 - is 180, so plus 180 is 1260... 1260 years." He sipped his soda mildly as Gregory smirked at his brainiac friend.

"How many days in a Hebrew month?" Fitz quizzed.

"30," Greg answered, jotting it down.

"What's 42 times 30?" Fitz asked. Gregory grabbed his calculator again and started entering the numbers, but again Jeremy's head is quicker.

"1260." Jeremy said.

"1260!" Gregory tosses his calculator down excitedly, "Then it's the same time prophecy in Revelation 11 and 13 as well!"

Fitz sat back and gave a satisfied smile as he tucked his hands behind his head and a glittering animation took over his screen. "Like the multiple surfaces of the same diamond - all revealing a different section of the same jewel. - Here, put it together and see what you get." He uses another animated sequence to illustrate. "Using the clues from all the time prophecies that refer to the 1260 days, what world power is different from the rest of the beasts before it, comes up from among the 10 horns, plucks up 3 of them, speaks blasphemy and persecutes the saints, causing them to have to go underground, and rules for 1,260 years?"

Gregory paused a second, "How would you define blasphemy?"

Fitz opened his Bible again, "My definition means nothing. Listen to what God defines it as - John 10:32 and 33, 'Jesus asked them, Many good works have I showed you from my Father; for which of those works do ye stone me? The Jews answered him, saying, For a good work we stone thee not; but for blasphemy; and because that thou, being a man, makest thyself God.' And here in Luke 5:20 and 21, when Jesus healed the paralytic man, He said, "Man, thy sins are forgiven thee. And the scribes and the Pharisees began to reason, saying, Who is this which speaketh blasphemies? Who can forgive sins, but God alone?'"

Jeremy looked puzzled, "Is there really someone on earth that claims to be God and claims to have the power to forgive sins?"

"Yes, there is, and we'll get to it in a moment," Fitz pressed another key on his computer and started a time line sequence superimposed over the 490 year prophecy and extending past. A slick animation of Emperor Justinian standing by a three-dimensional graphic reading the year '538 A.D.' appeared.

"Nice! Who is that?" Gregory leaned forward in his chair.

"The last Roman emperor, Justinian." Fitz adjusted his monitor so Gregory could see better. "After Justinian's rule, Rome was no longer the ruling world power, even though it still existed. Justinian had made all these elaborate laws uniting church and state under a one-world religion to try glue his crumbling empire back together - by the way, did you know that the word 'Catholic' means 'universal'?"

"No, I didn't know that." Gregory's appreciation for Fitz's study was growing.

"Yeah, actually the Justinian Codex is the basis for all European law." Jeremy added.

"Exactly," Fitz continued, "his point was to use it to unite church and state, making the state the enforcer of the church's dogma. That's why the pilgrims fled to America, but anyway, that ability and power had a starting point, right here, in 538, when Belisarius, Justinian's general, marched on Rome and took the city from the invading Ostrogoths. At that time, the Church of Rome accepted the exalted title 'THE HEAD OF ALL CHURCHES' as Justinian had decreed it should be called. She also accepted the persecuting policy Justinian had set up. He decreed her "throne" was a world power, the city of seven hills, where she sits today, with a pope on the throne that claims to be god on earth and who claims to have the power to forgive sins. And it's all here in Daniel and Revelation, hundreds of years before it happened."

"Amazing." Gregory was almost speechless.

"And 1,260 years from 538 is 1798." Jeremy pointed to a section of the line on the screen. Fitz initiated another animation, the time lines zipping by to an imposing picture of Napoleon.

"Right. The French Revolutionary Government asserted that the Roman Religion would always be a persistent enemy of the Republic, which is true, of course, because they are set up as a dictatorship. The government urged Napoleon to destroy the center of unity of the Roman church, and Napoleon did just that. In 1798, under his direction, the French general Berthier, with a French army, marched into Rome and proclaimed the political rule of the Papacy at an end and took the Pope prisoner. The Pope died in exile in France - the deadly wound to one of the beast's heads. At that time, the 1260 year worldwide rule of the Papacy was finished. History calls those 1260 years 'the dark ages' because they outlawed the Bible, the 'lamp unto our feet'."

"I think I'm beginning to get it – then the two witnesses prophesying in sackcloth for 1,260 days, the two olive trees holding the oil for the lamps in Revelation – "

"- are the word of God, the Old and New Testament, taken from the people for 1,260 years yet still speaking in sackcloth." Fitz finished Gregory's sentence excitedly. "They tried to kill them, to burn and destroy the Scriptures, but God raised them to life again through His faithful servants throughout all ages that protected their existence and worked, at the peril of their lives, to restore them to the world. It's all talking about this time." Fitz looked earnestly at Gregory, then checked his watch.

"It all makes so much sense." Gregory scribbled on his paper, but his pen had run out of ink. He quickly grabbed another one.

"Dude, we've got to get ready for class or we'll be late!" Jeremy quickly grabbed his things.

Gregory was reluctant for the time to end. "What about 1844?"

"Next time. But, you have to see, Gregory, that this is the most prophesied about time in the whole Bible. God doesn't want us to be confused about who the antichrist power is, what they do, what they stand for, or what their mark is. A merciful God would never announce wrath unmixed with mercy on anyone without giving them ample ability to escape it." Fitz ended his presentation on a detailed animation of Martin Luther uplifting the Scriptures.

Gregory stared at it pensively. "So, the separation was complete - Martin Luther understood the prophecies, and..."

Fitz finished his sentence, "found the assurance needed to stand for the truth, no matter what the cost." He took the jump drive from his computer and extended it toward Gregory in a silent challenge.

Greg met Fitz's unflinching gaze.

Chapter 12

~ On the Battlefield Again

Dr. Ribera watched as his class filed in, then stood up from behind his desk to walk to the center of the room and address them. Even though he was not very tall, his commanding appearance quieted the room quickly. His students gave him their full attention.

"Many of you have come to me, struggling with the final assignment. Thesis papers are no easy task," he paused for emphasis as he looked gravely at his students, "So, for class today, I would like to give you an opportunity to work on your papers during class time."

A wave of quiet relief and enthusiasm rolled through the class as he took his seat again at his desk. Gregory and Jeremy looked at each other. Jeremy was visibly relieved as he pulled out his crumpled paperwork and began writing. Gregory sat with a loaded expression, his Bible open to a verse.

Almost as an afterthought, Dr. Ribera added from his desk, "Those of you who would like to, can conference with me or fellow classmates during this time. The wise man said, 'in the multitude of counselors there is safety'."

Gregory sat up a little straighter and looked down at the verse his Bible was open to - Proverbs 11:14 *"Where no counsel is, the people fall: but in the multitude of counselors there is safety."* He glances at Jeremy who was watching him, puzzled. Greg stood, gripping his friend's shoulder briefly, and whispered, "Pray for me."

Dr. Ribera noticed him standing and asked, annoyed, "Gregory. What is it?"

Heart pounding, Gregory opened his mouth - nearly panicking when the words at first would not come out. "I - I would like to take this opportunity to present my thesis basis to the class - for peer review."

Dr. Ribera looked at him in silent suspicion. Then spoke slowly, riveting his piercing gaze on the trembling Gregory. "And... which one of your thesis topics would that be, Mr. Gregory?"

Gregory quickly picked up the stack of printed pages from his desk. "My key thought is from first

Peter, sir, chapter 4, verses 12 and 13. I - I haven't had much time to develop it and would appreciate the insight the class could give me."

Dr. Ribera scrutinized him carefully, then decided he seemed penitent enough. He glanced at his watch. "Ok. You have 15 minutes."

Relieved, Gregory took his laptop and walked toward the head of the class. He dropped a folded note onto Jeremy's desk as he passed by. Jeremy opened it and read it. *Pray for Courage - Luke 21:13-15.* Jeremy flipped quickly to the text and read it silently as Greg took his place nervously. *"And it shall turn to you for a testimony. Settle it therefore in your hearts, not to meditate before what ye shall answer: For I will give you a mouth and wisdom, which all your adversaries shall not be able to gainsay nor resist."*

Greg spread his papers out and plugged his laptop into the projector. He took out the large capacity jump drive Fitz had given him and plugged it in nervously, glancing at Fitz. Fitz nodded in encouragement as Gregory cleared his throat nervously, then took the white board marker from Dr. Ribera's outstretched hand. Dr. Ribera's stone face sent him a warning signal. He faltered and dropped the cap to the marker. Fumbling for it, he picked it up. The class was dead silent as he walked to the whiteboard and with trembling hand wrote "1 Peter 4:12 and 13" on the shiny surface. Dr. Ribera leaned back on his desk, arms folded. Gregory cleared his throat, then began with wobbly voice.

"At first, I thought my thesis should be about the mark of the beast. I worked pretty hard on it, but came to the realization that there is something more important to focus my energies on." He glanced over at Dr. Ribera, who leveled a hard, expectant stare at him with lifted brows. Gregory swallowed, then took a big, deep breath. "The trial of faith." He looked at Dr. Ribera again, who nodded his tentative approval as he moved to take his seat at his desk.

Gregory picked up his Bible and read from the open pages, "Beloved, think it not strange concerning the fiery trial which is to try you, as though some strange thing happened unto you: But rejoice, inasmuch as ye are partakers of Christ's sufferings; that, when his glory shall be revealed, ye may be glad also with exceeding joy." He looked at Jeremy, who was leaning forward in earnest, unsure of what was about to happen. "Some Bible scholars say the Bible writers wrote more about the last days than about their own time. I tend to agree with them."

He turned to the white board and drew a long line from left to right beneath the verse he wrote. "What I am about to show you, I only ask that you keep an open mind." He looked at Dr. Ribera again, who was seated forward tensely. He took another deep breath. "If you have your Bibles, it would be great if you could follow along." He wrote the following texts on the board as he was speaking - Daniel chapters 2, 7, 9, and 12, Revelation 13, 14, 16, 17, and 18.

Gaining courage he felt his voice strengthen. "In

Daniel 2, King Nebuchadnezzar has a prophetic dream about a statue whose head is of gold, arms and chest of silver, belly and thighs of brass, legs of iron, and feet of iron and clay. Then he sees a rock, cut without hands, smash it all to dust, and then fill the whole earth - what does it mean?"

A student in the back raises their hand. Gregory points to him to speak. "The chapter explains itself in Daniel's interpretation of the dream in the same chapter. It's a time prophecy. The kingdom of Babylon is the head of gold, the next kingdom to rule the world is Medo-Persia symbolized by the two arms, then Greece - they even used bronze shields, then Rome, the iron monarch, then the world was all divided, with no single 'world power'."

Gregory used his laptop graphics of the statue to illustrate the explanation. "Right, and each successive kingdom was more base, harder, less refined or civilized - just as each metal involved was less valuable."

Dr. Ribera interrupted testily as he glanced at his watch, "This is review, Mr. Gregory, - your time is almost up."

"Thank you sir, I'll hurry. Jumping to Daniel 7, Daniel has a prophetic dream about beasts - first, a winged lion, then a bear, raised up on one side, then a leopard with 4 heads and wings, then a 'dreadful and terrible beast with teeth of iron' and 10 horns. Three of the horns were uprooted by a new horn that has the eyes and mouth of a man that speaks great and blasphemous things. Then it says thrones were cast down and the Ancient of days sat down, and the judgment was set, then the beast was destroyed, and dominion was given to the Son of Man. What is that about?"

A voice called out from the back of the room in answer, "It's the same prophecy. The Bible explains itself in 7:17. The beasts are kingdoms - Babylon is the Lion this time, the wings show how fast they came into power, then the Bear with one high side is Medo-Persia, - like the two arms of the statue, one side stronger than the other, then the 4 headed leopard is Greece..." The student faltered a moment in his memory.

Fitz interrupted and continued the thought, "Alexander, King of Greece, died without naming a successor. They asked him who should rule after him, and he died saying 'the strongest'. All his generals fought to the death, and the kingdom ended up being divided between the 4 strongest generals."

The faltering student picked up the conversation again, "Out of one of them, the iron rule of Rome began, you know, the iron teeth, - and then came the 10 kingdoms of Europe - horns are powers, just like the 10 toes, with no dominating 'world power'."

Gregory glanced at Dr. Ribera who raised his eyebrows at him again testily. "Hold that thought and jump to Daniel 8 - the ram and the goat with the large horn between his eyes."

"The vision came in the last year of Babylon,"

another intrepid student ventured. The class was obviously enjoying the freedom of discussion. "Belshazzar was the last king of Babylon, so it skips Babylon and starts with Medo-Persia. The ram has 2 horns, like the 2 arms, and the bear with the raised shoulder - two shoulders. The goat is Greece - the single horn is Alexander."

"Daniel 8:20 and 21 explains itself. It says outright that the ram is Medo-Persia, and the goat is Greece." Fitz interjected again, reading from his Bible, "'And the great horn that is between his eyes is the first king'. Besides, the Greeks were known as Goat worshippers, the Goat of Mendes is associated with the pentagram, Pythagoras was an initiate into the mathematical cults of the time - remember Pan? Half goat half man deity? All from Greek mythology."

Dr. Ribera caught himself, surprised and intrigued. "That was not in class - where did you get that?"

"It's just history. I read up on it on the internet." Fitz shrugged.

Gregory glances at the clock seeing he is way past time, then seizes this opportunity of interest to keep going. "Right! Then what happens to the horns?"

"The goat and the ram fight, and the goat wins," another joined the discussion, "just as Greece won over Medo-Persia, but not long after that, the horn was broken - Alexander died at age 33 - and then 4 horns grew out of the place where the one horn was."

"Yes, again, because his 4 generals ruled after him, - after that comes up a little horn again that becomes great and does some terrible things. So, here is my question - considering these 3 prophecies all repeat the same thing, is it safe to assume that this little horn in Daniel 8 verse 9 is the same as the other little horn in Daniel 7 verse 8 that speaks blasphemous things in the other prophecy?"

The class was silent a second. Then one of the students ventured assertively, "Sure. That only makes sense."

Gregory began turning the pages of his Bible enthusiastically, "Look at Daniel 8:9-12. This little horn that comes up from the four winds of strife after Greece does some specific things - it waxes exceedingly great, even to the pleasant land - what land is more pleasant to Daniel than Israel? This horn, or power, pushes down and tries to crush out God's word and His people as a tyrant, right? Who is that?"

"Well, that's the antichrist, right?" Another student ventured a guess.

"I think it is." Gregory proposed innocently, "I mean, it would make sense considering the pattern, right?"

Dr. Ribera stood up, clearly ruffled, checking his watch and announcing firmly, "Well, that was a very nice review, Mr. Gregory. But I'm afraid your time is up."

Gregory looked with distress at Dr. Ribera, then at the class. Tension mounted as he stood firm. He did not want to return to his seat yet. The class was dead silent. Suddenly, a timid voice cleared his throat and spoke with slightly cracking tone.

"So - what's the point here?" Jeremy felt his color rising as he ventured bravely, giving Gregory half a smile for encouragement. Gregory smiled appreciatively back at his friend. Dr. Ribera saw he was losing control of the class as their interest was piqued. He strode over to Gregory and motioned for him to surrender the white board marker.

"Yeah, I mean, is that your thesis? I don't get it." Another student added.

"Yes, well it obviously needs work, doesn't it." Dr. Ribera responded tersely. "Maybe we can hear from someone who is a little further along in their development."

"Actually, there is a point, if I can just have a few more minutes..." Gregory pleaded.

Jeremy's voice cracked again as he piped up, "Does anyone object?"

There was a second of silence, then Fitz's firm voice ventured. "I'd like to hear what he has to say. I mean, you already laid a lot of ground work. What is your point here?"

The other students chorused their agreement, then looked expectantly at Dr. Ribera who stood awkwardly, trying not to appear as though he was strong-arming the situation. Finally he surrendered, unwillingly. "Well, if no one *else* wants to take advantage of this opportunity for help - this is the one and only time this opportunity for peer assistance will happen - you do realize this..." He tried to laugh lightly as he pressed his point home, but none of his students moved to rescue him. "Fine." He seated himself furiously at his desk as Gregory continued.

"Well, if the horn in Daniel 7 and 8 is the same horn, and it does the same thing that the antichrist does in Daniel 9, wouldn't it be logical that they are all taking about the same antichrist?" There was a general assent among the students. "Now let's take a quick look at those chapters in Revelation..."

The students began jumping ahead of him, reading the verses out loud excitedly.

"In Revelation 13, John sees a terrible beast, then a leopard, a bear, and a lion - the same thing as in Daniel's vision, just backward," an enthusiastic voice from the front called out.

Gregory began pacing as he talked excitedly, "Daniel was seeing the future. He was a Babylonian captive and lived to the rule of the Medes and Persians. John is seeing the past. He was a Roman prisoner. Rome was the ruling world power when he wrote Revelation. Keep your finger in Revelation 13, we're going back there."

"Revelation 17:3 says John saw in vision 'a woman sit upon a scarlet colored beast, full of names of

blasphemy, having seven heads and ten horns',"
Jeremy continued, flipping through his Bible.

"How many horns did the beast have in Daniel?"
Gregory asked.

"Ten. But I think it only had one head." A voice
answered from somewhere in the back of the room.

"Yes," another volleyed, "but the numbers are still
there - the 10 horns became 7, horns are powers,
heads are leaders."

"Repetition deepens impression," Gregory's face
was animated, "God repeats Himself and gives
more details each time. These are not separate
prophecies, all chopped up, - this is all one
prophecy, repeated and repeated because it
involves the most important warning in the whole
Bible - the only warning issued without mercy." He
paused for effect as the class sat on edge, including
Dr. Ribera, who was sitting at his desk, red-faced
and trying to restrain himself. Gregory took a deep
breath and read from his open Bible. "Revelation
14:9 and 10 - 'If any man worship the beast and his
image, and receive his mark in his forehead, or in
his hand, The same shall drink of the wine of the
wrath of God, which is poured out without mixture
of mercy into the cup of his indignation'." He put
his Bible down and looked solemnly at the class. "I
believe that there is enough information here to
find out who the beast is, and what his mark is."

After a tense moment, the class erupted into
excited discussion, some shaking their heads in
total disagreement, others thinking and wanting to

hear more. Dr. Ribera jumped to his feet and slammed his hand onto his desk in anger. "That is quite enough, Mr. Gregory." The doctor's face was beet red. "You may sit down or leave. The choice is yours. I will not tolerate your using my class as a platform for your outrageous theories and speculations. Moreover, this has nothing to do with your thesis topic, the trial of faith!" He pointed angrily to the text on the board.

"Sir, it has everything to do with it!" Gregory's face was twisted in passion. "Don't you see? It is *my* faith that is on trial here! If what I am about to prove is true - and I believe it is - it changes everything!"

"You are full of yourself! God resisteth the proud!" Dr. Ribera hissed.

"Feed the flock of God which is among you, not by constraint, but willingly; not for filthy lucre," Gregory's penetrating honest stare made the doctor lower his eyes a moment, "but of a ready mind; Neither as being lords over God's heritage, but being ensamples to the flock. Are you more interested in bowing to your donors for the college, or teaching Bible students what the Bible actually says?"

Fitz's gaze flickered interestedly as he met Dr. Ribera's eyes. For a moment Dr. Ribera stood speechless, then regained his disdain-filled postulating. "You are out of line, Gregory Martin!"

Gregory turned to the class and cried out passionately, "Study to show thyself approved unto

God, a workman that needeth not to be ashamed, rightly dividing the word of truth!"

A wave of support surged as the class erupted into loud dissensions and discussions. Fitz watched silently as Gregory battled for his voice to be heard. After a moment, Fitz tipped his head to the side curiously and spoke quietly, but loud enough to catch the professor's ear. "I'd like to hear what he has to say." Dr. Ribera glared at him, red faced. Fitz didn't flinch as he continued calmly, "It's still a free county, right? Freedom of speech?"

Dr. Ribera sat down at his desk furiously, then glared at Gregory to continue. A frazzled Greg nodded his thanks toward Fitz and tried to regain his composure.

"So, who is the beast, and what do you think his mark is?" Fitz probed.

Gregory took a deep breath and continued, "Jeremiah 6:16 says 'Thus saith the LORD, Stand ye in the ways, and see, and ask for the old paths, where is the good way, and walk therein, and ye shall find rest for your souls.'" The students settle down and watch him silently. "Would we be safe if we went with what Peter or Paul believed? Or John?" Some of the students nod to each other, others shrug. The thought seems safe and logical. Gregory paces slowly as he unfolds his argument with intense drama. "In first Peter chapter 4 verse 7, Peter says 'the *end of all things* is at hand: be ye therefore sober, and watch unto prayer.' Paul, when he was writing to the church at Corinth said 'Now all these things ... are written for our admonition, *upon whom the ends of the world are come*' - so they both believed they were living in the time of the end. Daniel 12:9 says the prophesies are shut up *until the time of the end.* Revelation begins and ends with the same shocking statement in chapter 1 verse 3: 'Blessed is he that readeth, and they that hear the words of this prophecy, and keep those things which are written therein: *for the time is at hand.*' So John also believed the end time had begun in his day. At the end of Revelation, the angel says to John 'Seal *not* the sayings of the prophecy of this book: for *the time is at hand.*' - and we have seen that the prophecies are the same as those in Daniel - the closed book was now open, in John's day, the end time. So that can mean only one thing..." He looked around the room at the solemn faces staring back at him. "If the antichrist is to appear in the end times, and the Bible shows the last days has already started in John's day and Paul and Peter's day, *then he is already here.*"

The class gasped and whispers started. Greg quietly regained their interest as he continued softly. "What world power reigned after Greece?"

"Rome," one of the students answered.

"And who reigned after Rome?" The class looked silently at each other.

"Who?" Someone asked.

Gregory turned to the image from Nebuchadnezzar's dream projected on the board. "The legs are the longest part of the body, and Rome had the longest reign of any superpower in the prophecy in Daniel 2. Rome persecuted the church relentlessly, first under the Caesars.... and then..."

The realization of the implication hit one of the students seated in front of the class and it showed on his shocked expression as he took a breath and answered, almost to himself, "...under the popes. In the dark ages."

"Yes," Gregory answered, elated that the message was being understood. He continued, excitedly. "It was a Roman death warrant that put Christ to death. His death ended God's acceptance of the sacrifices and offerings because Jesus was the ultimate offering, the One all the lambs pointed forward to. Then, at the destruction of Jerusalem, the Romans destroyed the city, and the temple, the sanctuary, trampling it and all the truth it holds, underfoot. Now, what does a woman represent in Bible prophecy?"

"A church," Fitz responded, enjoying seeing the interest piqued. "God likens His people to a comely woman. When they were unfaithful to Him, He likens them to a harlot."

"In Revelation 17, that beast, Rome, has a harlot riding it, controlling it." Gregory brought up one of Fitz's graphics in illustration.

"So, what are you saying?" Another student queried.

"What I say doesn't matter," Gregory lifted his Bible into the air, "Let's look at history and the Bible. Rome's temple of worship was called the

Pantheon. Rome, like many pagan nations before it, had a habit of collecting the gods of the nations it conquered. Rome at this time was crumbling. Their oppressive rule, the antagonism between the religious sects, and their failing economy led them to make one last acquisition to try to glue the country together - they made an agreement with the strengthening Christian church, and enveloped them into their Pantheon, with all their other gods and pagan systems and rites, hoping to bring together a crumbling kingdom by instituting religious unity. Thus was born the *Roman Catholic* - meaning 'universal' - church. The institution born of the compromise between Christianity and paganism. Eventually, the Roman church took over the Roman Empire. Even the emperors began looking to Rome for guidance. The popes could end the rule of an emperor, and did, whenever they wanted to. That's what John and Daniel meant when they called the last beast 'diverse' from the others - because it was the only one that was a religio-political power."

"Wait a minute - are you saying that - that ROME is the antichrist?" An incredulous student blurted out.

"No." Gregory answered firmly. "Martin Luther, and the early reformers asserted that the Roman church, the Catholic system, is. This knowledge is what gave them the courage to stand up for what they believe. I am agreeing with them though. When pagan Rome became Papal Rome, it merely added Christ to their pagan collection. The compromise on both sides was gradual. Books were not common, and ignorance prevailed. Those who knew the Scriptures and the early disciples easily pointed out the errors and warned the people. But as the Bible was removed from society, locked up under the pretense that common people were not educated enough to understand what God was revealing in His word, people forgot what God said, and the priests had an easy time getting them to believe and do as the church wanted. They had almost absolute power. But God didn't leave His people in darkness. He raised up reformers, like Wycliff and Luther, who restored the Bible to the people, in their own language. As people began studying for themselves, they saw the corruption in the church, and moved to reform the church, or escape it. That is why there was such a big division between the reformers and the Roman Church! Though there are many good Christians in the Catholic Church, the system, like pagan Rome, its predecessor, is *anti*-christ. That's why God says to us in Revelation 18:4, 'come out of her, My people.' That is why we are *protest*-ants. The pilgrims came to America to protest against Roman Catholic rule that would not allow them to believe - or not believe, according to their own consciences. That is why freedom of religion is one of the very first freedoms guaranteed by the constitution, because they knew what it was like to be oppressed. But we have forgotten."

Dr. Ribera sneered at Gregory, annoyed, "Mr. Gregory, this is a prophecy class, not American history. What is the relevance here?"

"Yes," added Fitz, not wanting Gregory to lose his advantage. "And where does the seven year tribulation and secret rapture fit into all this?"

"Actually, it doesn't," Gregory answered, "And I can prove it, Biblically, by the time prophecies."

"I'd like to see that," a student on the front said, genuinely interested.

"But the Bible says He will come as a thief in the night," another student challenged.

"Have you ever read that whole verse, in context, and just let the word speak for itself?" Gregory challenged in return. The sound of pages turning filled the room, followed by silence. "Second Peter 3:10," Gregory began quoting as they read along, "'But the day of the Lord will come as a thief in the night; in the which the heavens shall pass away with a great noise, and the elements shall melt with fervent heat, the earth also and the works that are therein shall be burned up.' Does that sound like there are any survivors at His coming? It was like a thief, - because it was surprising, unanticipated. How about first Thessalonians 5 verses 2 through 4?"

Jeremy read out loud, "For yourselves know perfectly that the day of the Lord so cometh as a thief in the night. For when they shall say, Peace and safety; then sudden destruction cometh upon them, as travail upon a woman with child; and they shall not escape. But ye, brethren, are not in darkness, that that day should overtake you as a thief."

Gregory pulled up a graphic illustration of the end of the world. "The world *ends* when Jesus comes again. There is no second chance. The time to choose whom we will serve is now, just like during the flood when Noah was preaching, those who refused to enter the ark perished in the flood. No second chance. When people think they have a second chance, they don't take advantage of the present opportunities." He searched the faces of his fellow students as he continued earnestly, "How many people have you spoken to, sharing the word, who have said to you, 'When I see the Christians disappear, then I'll get my act together and believe'? Jesus likens the end of the world to the destruction of Sodom and Gomorrah. Where was their second chance? The Bible says, Now is the day of salvation. If today you hear His voice, harden not your heart. Telling people they have a second chance that doesn't exist is a deadly deception that results in one thing - loss of souls."

"Get to your point." Dr. Ribera snapped, "You are trying my patience."

Gregory paused as he considered Dr. Ribera's open hostility. Then he looked at Fitz who nodded an encouragement to him. A war was raging in his heart and mind. How far could he go in his separation from all that was familiar to him? He glanced at Jeremy. His head was bowed and his lips were moving silently. Gregory knew he was praying for courage – for him. With trembling heart and sweaty palms he continued. "When Daniel was in Babylon, he was thrown into the lion's den for refusing to break God's first law, to have no other gods before the God of heaven. His friends were thrown into the fiery furnace for refusing to bow down to an idol. Babylon is known historically for making laws that are against God's laws with death penalties attached."

Fitz read out loud, "And he causeth all, both small and great, rich and poor, free and bond, to receive a mark in their right hand, or in their foreheads: And that no man might buy or sell, save he that had the mark, or the name of the beast, or the number of his name. Revelation 13:16 and 17."

"Those who take that mark, are thrown into the lake of fire," Gregory continued, "'And the smoke of their torment ascendeth up forever and ever: and they have no rest day nor night, who worship the beast and his image, and whosoever receiveth the mark of his name.' Those who don't are described right after that in Revelation 14:12 as those 'that keep the commandments of God, and the faith of Jesus.'"

"So... which commandment is it going to be?" another voice asked.

"The *one* that Papal Rome claims is the *'mark'* of her authority. I'll let them tell you - in their own words." Gregory pulled out a folded paper from his jacket and read from it, "Question - Which is the Sabbath day? Answer - Saturday is the Sabbath day. Question - Why do we observe Sunday instead of Saturday? Answer - We observe Sunday instead of Saturday because the Catholic Church, in the Council of Laodicea A.D. 364, transferred the solemnity from Saturday to Sunday. Peter Geiermann, C.S.S.R., The Convert's Catechism of Catholic Doctrine, page 50, third edition, 1957." He put down the page and began bringing up quotes on his laptop, shining them on the wall through the projector and reading them out loud to the silent class. "'You may read the Bible from Genesis to Revelation, and you will not find a single line authorizing the sanctification of Sunday. The Scriptures enforce the religious observance of Saturday, a day which we never sanctify. James Cardinal Gibbons, The Faith of Our Fathers, 1917 edition, page 72 and 73, 16th edition, page 111, 88th edition, page 89. 'Most Christians assume that Sunday is the biblically approved day of worship. The Catholic Church protests that *it* transferred Christian worship from the biblical Sabbath, which is Saturday, to Sunday, and that to try to argue that the change was made in the Bible is both dishonest and a denial of Catholic authority. If Protestantism wants to base its teachings only on the Bible, it should worship on Saturday. Rome's Challenge, Dec 2003. I have a lot more references if you'd like to see them." He lifted a stack of copied papers onto the desk as several nearby students grabbed them and began passing them around.

"This is outrageous!" No longer able to contain himself, Dr. Ribera leaped out of his chair.

Gregory's courage rose up afresh as he made his answer, holding his Bible and reading the verses he had highlighted, "Not really. Satan's issue was that he wanted to be like God. He said, 'I will ascend into heaven, I will exalt my throne above the stars of God, I will ascend above the heights of the clouds; I will be like the most High.' Isaiah 14:13, 14. God has a mark - it's a protective mark, and those who receive God's mark show their allegiance to Him by keeping the institution He has set up as their Creator Redeemer. And He tells us what it is in Exodus 31:13: 'Surely My Sabbaths you shall keep, for *it* is a *sign* between me and you throughout your generations that you may know that I am the Lord.' Ezekiel 9:4-6 says 'The LORD said unto the angel with the writer's inkhorn, Go through the midst of the city of Jerusalem, and set a *mark* upon the foreheads of the men that sigh and that cry for all the abominations that be done in the midst thereof, And to the others he said, Go ye after him through the city, and slay utterly old and young, both maids, and little children, and women: but come not near any man upon whom is the mark; and begin at my sanctuary.' So the antichrist, who is the arch deceiver and wants to be like God, has a mark too. And he works through any that are willing to let him, even professed Christian religions who make the mistake of trying to exercise Babylonian power. The Catholic church says this, 'Sunday is our mark of authority. The church is above the Bible, and this transference of Sabbath observance is proof of that fact.' The Catholic Record, London, Ontario, September 1, 1923." The class rippled with comments.

"So, are you saying we all have the mark of the beast?" Fitz asked calmly.

"Is there a law that prohibits all but those who worship on Sunday to buy and sell?" Gregory answered. "No. That has not happened, so, no, the mark is not here - yet. But it's coming." He pulled up another set of quotes on the screen. "'The civil authorities should be urged to cooperate with the church in maintaining and strengthening this public worship of God, and to support with their own authority the regulations set down by the church's pastors. For it is only in this way that the faithful will understand why it is Sunday and not the Sabbath day that we now keep holy.' Roman Catechism, 1985. They can't explain their position of enforcement from the Bible, because as even they admit, 'Sunday is a Catholic institution and its claim to observance can be defended only on Catholic principles..... From beginning to end of Scripture there is not a single passage that warrants the transfer of weekly public worship from the last day of the week to the first.' Catholic Press, Sydney, Australia. But this is a protestant nation, so they begin their indoctrination in their attempt to unify the nations under their religious banner by introducing it softly, gently, maybe as a family day, so the next steps - laws and enforcement, will seem logical and more supportable. But the issues will be unveiled before the world. The mark of the beast is in the hand or forehead, because it can be taken by mental ascent as signified by the forehead, or just by appearances, or convenience by submitting to the Roman Church power instead of the God of heaven, as signified by the mark in the hand. But God is satisfied with the heart only. His mark is only on the forehead. He wants us to choose Him, not by default, but by love and through knowing Him and His word. Before Daniel was thrown to the lions, God used him in a powerful way to interpret the dream of Nebuchadnezzar. God ensured that the entire realm of Babylon knew who Daniel was and what he stood for, so when the test came, all the princes and people knew the issues that were at stake. It was the same with his friends in the furnace. That very statue they were to bow down to was made in defiance of God's revealed prophecy that the great city of Babylon would one day fall, that's why they made the whole thing of gold instead of just the head. God is not unfair - He brings the issues to the forefront first, then He calls us to 'choose this day whom we will serve', and then, and only then, once people have had an opportunity to make their decisions for or against the truth, judgment comes."

"Much learning doth make thee mad." Dr. Ribera shot angrily.

"The king knoweth of these things, before whom also I speak freely: for I am persuaded that none of these things are hidden from him; for this thing was not done in a corner." Gregory parried. Dr. Ribera's face registered a moment of thought.

"Almost thou persuadest me..." He said softly to himself as though repeating something he was hearing in his mind.

"I would to God, that not only thou, but also all that hear me this day, were both almost, and altogether such as I am, - except these bonds." Gregory glanced at the doctoral plaque on the wall with the school's name on it. Dr. Ribera's face hardened again. The class sat in stunned silence, the impact of the words registering on each face. "If I am right, and I believe I am - because this is what Martin Luther himself believed, as well as many other great reformers, then we have a lot of studying to do. Don't we?"

As if on cue, the buzzer sounded and the class was over. The students stood and shuffled out, talking excitedly about what they heard. Gregory gathered his things slowly and turned to go, glancing at Dr. Ribera, and expecting to be asked to stay behind. He paused at his desk a moment, but Dr. Ribera merely smiled at him cruelly.

One of the students from the front row left his discussion with Fitz and jostled his way to where Gregory was joining the flow of students leaving the class. "Hey. I think you are right on. And so does my dad. Our family has been a major supporter of this school for generations, and the rapture theory wasn't always what was taught here - only in the last 50 years or so. We've been studying it out. A lot of us have. I'm just surprised that someone actually had the guts to stand up and say something." He turned to go, leaving Gregory encouraged, but speechless as he watched his figure retreat into the surge of bodies.

Chapter 13

~ Counterattack

Gregory was sitting quietly in his chair, working on his paper when Jeremy came in. He paused a moment, watching Gregory wordlessly, silently tracing the words on one of his aeronautics books.

"How can you be so sure?" he finally ventured, "You're banking everything on being right, you know."

"Sometimes you just have to go with what you believe, what is important to you." Gregory looked at his friend. "It's hard to stand alone - to go against the flow."

"Because somebody tells you to?"

"No, because I've studied it out. That's what God wants us to do. Study things out for ourselves. That's what we have the Bible for."

Jeremy looked at him flatly, then at his untouched Bible sitting dustily under a heap of other books and magazines. Gregory reached for it, pulling it out from the pile, and gently placed it on top as he continued gently. "We have to start putting what God says above what man says. He makes sense, He is not arbitrary or vindictive - He speaks so simply even a child can understand Him. He wants us to think - to understand. That is why in Isaiah He says, 'come, let us reason together'."

Jeremy looked steadily at Gregory, his brow furrowed in thought.

~

With flourish, Dr. Ribera wrote on the white board as he stood in front of his tense students. "Sunday sacredness - Biblical support" and the six texts below it spoke silently in bold letters: Matt 28:1; Mark 16:2, 9; Luke 24:1; John 20:1, 19; Acts 20:7; 1 Cor. 16:2. With an air of authority he stood at the head of his class, capping his marker. Jeremy and Gregory squirmed uneasily in their seats. Dr. Ribera regarded them with reticent disdain.

"To avoid the confusion caused by the recent presentation of Gregory's theory, we will be re-grounding ourselves in the Biblical truth of Sunday sacredness," He basked in his perceived superiority and feeling of power. "Colossians 2:16, 17 says, 'Let no man therefore judge you in meat, or in drink, or in respect of an holyday, or of the new moon, or of the sabbath days, which are a shadow of things to come; but the body is of Christ'."

A ruffle of whispers rippled through the class. Gregory shot a look at Jeremy, who looked confused as he shrugged.

"All of the sabbaths in the old testament were shadows of what Jesus would do when He came." Dr. Ribera indulged in a self satisfied smirk as he caught Gregory's distress, "For example, the Jewish feast day sabbaths - the day of atonement, and first fruits, and the days of unleavened bread."

Gregory shifted again in his seat, wanting to refute the text as he flipped through his Bible, fingers in several places. Irritated, Dr. Ribera purposefully ignored his upraised hand and called on a different student.

"How is the Sabbath in the 10 commandments a shadow?" Gregory was surprised as he turned to see that the speaker was someone he didn't know.

Dr. Ribera's irritation was quickly rising. "It is a shadow of what Jesus would do when He came to earth. He kept the law."

"So we don't have to?" Another voice chipped in.

"Yes - well, no," Dr. Ribera loosened his tie as he was caught bumbling for words, "We do have to keep them, but only in spirit. Not in actuality. That is why it is the spirit of the day, not the actual day that matters."

"So, as long as I love my neighbor as I am murdering him, I am ok?" The first student joked as the class snickered.

Dr. Ribera raised his voice defiantly, "The Sabbath as an institution is perpetual - the day does not matter. It was originally Saturday, in honor of the creation, but now is Sunday, in honor of the resurrection. Pentecost and the ascension were all on the first day of the week - not on the Sabbath!"

"Isn't that because it was business as usual on a regular day? On Saturday Jesus rested in the tomb, and his disciples rested 'according to the commandment', not even embalming their beloved Lord's body in the tomb, on Sabbath." Gregory marveled as he heard logical arguments coming from the mouths of students he had never met.

"Jesus especially honored the first day by manifesting himself to them on four separate occasions after the crucifixion." Dr. Ribera raised himself up as high as his small stature would allow, trying to assert his authority.

"All four of those times that Jesus appeared to His disciples on Sunday, except one, were on the same day - the first Sunday after the crucifixion Friday," The anonymous student continued as he contended. "It only makes sense that he went to show himself to them so they could see that he was risen as He said. They were scared, hiding in a upper room. The last appearance in your texts, in John 20, was the next Sunday, when Thomas was there. He was missing the first time."

"The disciples understood it to mean that the day had changed, that is why they met on Sunday from then on." Dr. Ribera hissed, his short temper besting him.

Gregory flipped quickly through his Bible and raised his hand eagerly only to be overlooked again as Dr. Ribera called on a student somewhere behind him.

Referring to his Bible, the student replied, "Over nine times in Acts, it says they still met on Sabbath. In Acts 18:4 it says 'Paul reasoned in the synagogue *every* Sabbath day' - "

"Acts 20:7 says that upon the first day of the week, when the disciples came together to break bread, Paul preached unto them," interrupted Dr. Ribera impatiently.

The student continued reading from the text, "...'ready to depart on the morrow; and continued his speech until midnight.' The Biblical reckoning of a day starts at night, like in Genesis, where it says 'the evening and the morning were the first day.' This meeting with Paul would be an evening meal on what we would call Saturday night, like a vespers meeting, before Paul left Sunday morning, to continue business as usual. And just because someone preaches on a day doesn't make it the Sabbath, or Wednesday night prayer meetings would be Sabbaths too."

The class snickered.

"Paul endorsed Sunday sacredness in 1 Corinthians

16 when he told the people that 'Upon the first day of the week let every one of you lay by him in store, as God hath prospered.' This is the gathering of tithes and offerings at a church service." Even Dr. Ribera's eyebrows were raised as he attempted to tower over his students.

"He actually explains himself in that chapter as well," someone else continued respectfully, "He was on his way to Macedonia, and wrote to the Corinthian church the same thing he wrote to the church in Galatia - that he would be in Ephesus until Pentecost, then would travel through Macedonia to Corinth, where he wanted to pick up the donations for the saints in Jerusalem to show their support of the church - remember there was a lot of friction between the gentile and the Jewish Christians and the offering was a token of their support and unified interests. He wanted the offerings ready to pick up quickly because he was trying to beat the winter storms which made sea travel very dangerous. To wait for the believers to gather the funds would delay the trip. From Corinth, he was sending the money with trustworthy friends to Jerusalem, even though he himself wintered in Corinth."

"The disciples themselves accomplished this change by worshipping on Sunday in honor of the resurrection!" Dr. Ribera hissed.

"Which disciples were those? I don't remember reading about them in my Bible." Someone retorted.

"It is a simple historical fact, beginning around 300 AD. Look it up." Dr. Ribera stated as he tried to reign in his raging temper.

"If you mean those who were worshipping on Sunday after AD 321 when Constantine passed a law saying all who do not worship on the 'venerable day of the Sun' you are probably correct. But that does not make it God's new day of worship. God has revealed which day is His, and if He wanted to change it, I'm sure He would make it very clear that He had." Gregory marveled at the firmness of the speaker and the number of those who agreed with what he fought to present. He had felt alone, but God had been working in others' hearts to bring light from the Scriptures just as much as in his own.

"Are you denying the validity of the custom of the early church?" Dr. Ribera was fast losing the desire and ability to restrain his anger.

"I stand on my Bible alone." A brave student answered.

Dr. Ribera looked around the class, his eyes glittering with hostility. "How the seeds of doubt have been sown and do spring up, bearing fruit of rebellion, disorder, and confusion."

"With all due respect, the exercise of freedom of conscience is not rebellion, sir, but a God-given right." A somber voice answered.

~

1563 A.D.

The council of Trent is in full swing under the auspices of Pope Pius IV. By now, the anti-Protestant Jesuits have become a formidable force, convened specifically for the destruction of Protestantism and the establishment of the strength of the Catholic Church. The stated purpose of the council was to condemn the principles and doctrines of Protestantism and to clarify the doctrines of the Catholic Church on all disputed points, and to assert that the Church is the ultimate interpreter of Scripture, and the Bible and Church Tradition (not mere customs but the ancient tradition that made up part of the Catholic faith) were equally authoritative.

"Your time has expired. You are required to make your decision. Will you adhere to your absurd declaration of 'Scripture alone'? Or agree with your mother church that truth is determined upon tradition *and* the Scripture?" The Archbishop Reggio addressed the disparaging reformers who stood before the council as emissaries of their creed.

The reformers look despairingly at each other, then their pale and haggard spokesperson stood and spoke haltingly.

"Archbishop Reggio, Venerable council, deign to point out to us wherein we have erred."

"You must revoke all your errors, and embrace the true doctrine of the Church!" The Archbishop shouted belligerently.

"We ask for *Scripture*; it is on Scripture alone that our faith is founded." The Reformer bowed his head respectfully as he opened his hands in humble suppliance.

"Do you not know that the Pope is above all?" The haughty Archbishop raised his chin defiantly.

"Not above Scripture." The emissary's tone was firm but gentle.

"Yes, above Scripture, and above councils!" Archbishop Reggio lost restraint and his intolerance was revealed. His voice raised to a fever pitch as he screamed, "Retract, retract! For it is hard for you to kick against the pricks!"

"Our conscience remains bound by the Word of God." The Reformer paled, but his tone remained firm.

The Archbishop cast a significant look, nearly a smile, to a dark robed monk who stepped forward and spoke in a heavily accented but smooth tone, "Well, dear, Protestants, you could never defend Sunday sacredness, for if you continue to offer as your authority the Bible and the Bible only, it is clear that you have no Bible command for the first day of the week." Pallavicini smiled magnanimously at them in their bewilderment.

Archbishop Reggio smiled cruelly as he pressed his advantage against the divided Reformers, "It is then evident that the church has power to change the commandments because by its power alone, and not by the preaching of Jesus, it had transferred the Sabbath from Saturday to Sunday. None of you can continue to fight the acceptance of tradition when the only authority for Sunday sacredness in the church *is* tradition."

The reformers quietly counseled together as they searched wearily through their Bibles to no avail, and the papal representatives gloated triumphantly. Finally their shoulders fell in defeat as they regarded their fierce adversaries.

"It's not there, dear friends," Pallavicini coddled, "Take all the time you need to search. In the end you will find that there is *no scriptural authority* for the change. Tradition is of equal authority with the Sacred Scriptures. Therefore, the priests only, and not the laity, are capable of rightly interpreting the Scriptures." He laughed gently at their despairing looks, then turned toward the Pope seated on this throne.

"See, your holiness," he mocked, "these Reformers, these 'protesters' of Rome, love to hide behind their Bibles, hurling insults and gloating on their position of 'sola scriptura' –"

"- But where is their Scripture now?" Archbishop Reggio smirked surreptitiously as he completed the thought.

A paige jogged over from the reformers with a note for the prelate.

"The Reformers request a short recess for deliberation," he reported respectfully.

The archbishop shot a look of triumph to the pope.

"We have them!"

The pope smiled graciously and nodded his assent to the request.

~

James Todd was seated at his desk as Dr. Ribera entered with Gregory's paper and tossed it onto his desk in frustration.

"The boy is as stubborn as a mule!" He dropped himself into one of the plush chairs as he vented, "His insurrection is infecting the entire student body. He must be stopped!"

James Todd picked up the papers and scanned them briefly, then slammed them down on his desk in frustration, rubbing his forehead. "This little Martin Luther want-to-be will *not* cost the school its grant." He picked up his phone and dialed an internal extension. "Dean Bellarmine, please bring me Gregory Martin's records and personal file."

~

Gregory knocked at the open door of Professor Schwarzerd's office. He was grading papers at his desk, and Gregory hoped to speak to him alone. The professor smiled when he saw him standing in the doorway.

"Gregory, come in! What can I do for you?" the

professor's warm, fatherly manner was a balm to Gregory's chaffed spirit.

"Professor Schwarzerd, you've always told us that God makes sense. He is not arbitrary or vindictive - He speaks so simply that even a child can understand Him," Gregory began hesitantly, not knowing where to start. "He wants us to think - to understand. That is why in Isaiah He says, 'come, let us reason together', right?"

Professor Schwarzerd looked at him kindly as he cut to the heart of the matter. "This is about your prophecy thesis?"

A surprised look flitted across Gregory's face. He hadn't realized the controversy was so well known. He stared at his shoes. "Am I wrong? Everyone is telling me that I am tearing the school apart."

"I think you are struggling with the balance between grace and the law, Gregory." The professor smiled kindly. "All good students of the gospel do at some point."

"Sir?" Gregory could sense the encouragement, but was unsure of the message as he guarded himself against the compliment.

"The Bible defines sin as the transgression of the law, 1 John 3:4, right? What law?" Professor Schwarzerd asked.

"The ten commandments, I guess."

"So, what law did Adam and Eve break in the

garden? 'Thou shalt not eat of the tree' is not part of the 10 commandments."

"No. But - there *is* a commandment that says 'thou shalt have no other gods before me' - Romans 6:16 'to whom you yield yourselves servants to obey, his servants ye are to whom ye obey; whether of sin unto death, or of obedience unto righteousness'. God said 'don't eat it', Satan through the serpent said, 'eat it', and we show our allegiance to the master we obey." Gregory pressed his point home in earnest.

"Exactly!" A puzzled look filled Gregory's face at the professor's unexpected statement of agreement. "So, then the Ten Commandments were always there, they didn't just 'appear' at Sinai during the Exodus." Intrigued, Gregory watched as the professor clicked open his laptop and pulled up a chart with texts and references regarding God's character and the character of the law. "I wanted to show you this study I completed a few years ago. All through the Bible it compares the Law to God - God is good, God is just, God is holy, then it says the law is holy, just and good. You can find this over and over throughout Scripture."

Gregory studied the chart a moment. "Wow! That's clear. I'd like to have that..."

The professor smiled as he typed quickly. "I just emailed you a copy for yourself." Gregory sat down at a nearby desk. "Gregory, God called everything He created 'good' in the beginning. He called the forbidden tree 'the tree of the knowledge of good *and* evil'. When we ate of that tree, as a race, we no longer experienced only the good God had for us, but also the evil His enemy wanted to bring on us, and our moral compass was destroyed. We don't know what right and wrong is a lot of times, so, after sin, God 'quantified' what good was in His 10 laws - laws that were always there, because they define what good is." Gregory's brow furrowed as he contemplated the thought. "How do you change God's law, Gregory? Since the law is a transcript of God's character, it is who He is, and is the foundation of His government. God says He does not change, so to change the law you'd have to climb up to heaven and change God Himself!" Professor Schwarzerd sat forward eagerly as he delved into his subject, "Think about it, if the law could be changed, then why did Jesus have to die? He died for our sins to fulfill the requirements of the law - the law says the wages of sin is death."

"This is where I am the most confused sir, because if He fulfilled the law, it should no longer apply to us, right?"

The professor picked up his Bible and quickly flipped to a text, "Does fulfill mean destroy? Matthew 5:17 - 'Think not that I am come to destroy the law, or the prophets: I am not come to destroy, but to ...destroy?' No, he said 'fulfill'. Can we now with impunity kill, steal, and disrespect our parents because Jesus died for our sins? Does that make any sense at all? The fact Jesus *died* in our place is proof that the law still stands. His death on our behalf shows that we were condemned because of our transgression of the law. The penalty was transferred from us to Him, that we might live. Jesus would not have had to pay the price for our transgression otherwise. The law, still intact, then demands our obedience. 'Do we then make void the law through faith? God forbid: yea, we establish the law.' Romans 3:31. This is also impossible for us to accomplish. Our salvation then is through God's grace alone. We don't keep the law of ourselves, we cannot. 'I am crucified with Christ: nevertheless I live; yet not I, but Christ liveth in me: and the life which I now live in the flesh I live by the faith of the Son of God, who loved me, and gave himself for me.' Galatians 2:20. Just as we rely on Jesus' death for us to pay the penalty for our sin, we rely on His keeping of the law to fulfill the righteousness of the law on our behalf. And as we behold Him doing this on our behalf, we are changed into His image – He remakes us, restores Himself in us, as the Author and finisher of our faith. So we are saved by His death, yes, but even moreso by His life. We are saved by His grace, and as we grow up in Christ, He establishes His ten promises in us through the working of His Holy Spirit in our hearts. 'Thou shalt not kill' – because we love. 'Thou shalt not steal' – because we love. We would keep the fourth commandment because we love Him who first loved us and set aside a special day for us to spend with our Creator. Our keeping the law then is the measure of the transformation of the creature - merely doing what it was created to do, merely following the shepherd, Jesus, who never sinned, leaving us an example to follow. It is the proof of our being born again, and the measure of our surrender to our new Master."

His watch timer went off and he checked the time quickly and began gathering his things. Gregory stood with him as they walked out of the classroom. "You know, a wise reformer once said, 'We teach best what we need to learn most'. I was an atheist when I first started teaching here," He chuckled at the memory as he locked his classroom door. "I often asked why I had to land my first teaching job in a Christian school. We had a baby on the way and I needed work so badly. We don't always understand the shepherd's leading, son. He never promised the way would be easy, but He did promise He would be with us, always, and that if we could see the way as He sees it, from the beginning to the end, we would choose no other way than the one He has marked out for us... I may never make tenure. But, my God shall provide all my needs." Professor Schwarzerd put a comforting hand on Gregory's shoulder. "Gregory, when is the seeming majority ever right in this world?" He smiled and disappeared down the hall leaving Gregory standing pensively with his thoughts.

Suddenly he had the feeling he was not alone in the eerie silence of the quiet classrooms. He looked up and down the hall, but saw no one as he turned uneasily down the hall, his footsteps echoing on the polished floors. Then he noticed the rigid features of the dean in the reflection of one of the glass doors, as he watched him with steely eyes. Then he disappeared, leaving Gregory feeling strangely shaken.

Long into the night he lay in bed, staring at the ceiling as he turned things over thoughtfully in his mind.

Chapter 14

~ The Donkey Speaks Again

Greg stood outside the laundromat, carefully watching for the dean. Finally he saw Melanie come out from the back room with an armload of clothes to fold. He glanced both ways, then entered.

Melanie looked up from her work briefly, then ignored him as she continued folding. He caught Missy's eye as she smiled shyly and returned his little wave. She grabbed onto her mom's leg and patted her repeatedly to get her attention while pointing at Greg.

"Mommy, mommy, mommy - look - " She patted her mother on her leg over and over again.

Melanie finally put her hands on her hips and looked down at her daughter. "Missy, stop. I know. I see him, but mommy's mad at Gregory right now and she is not speaking to him, ok? So let's just keep folding. Play with your blocks, sweetie."

Gregory saw his opportunity and stepped forward. "Hey Missy - if you see your mom, can you tell her something for me?"

Missy looks at him puzzled, a little smile playing on her cute lips as she caught onto the game. She looked up at her mom then nodded at Gregory.

"Do you know the story about Balaam in the Bible?"

Missy shook her head.

"Well, this man, Balaam, wasn't doing what God wanted him to do, and he wasn't listening when God was speaking to him. So, God did an amazing thing - do you want to know what that was?"

Missy smiles and nodded.

"He used a donkey to talk to him - then he finally listened. Have you ever heard a donkey talk?"

Missy giggled and shook her head again.

"Me neither. But when you see your mommy, maybe you can tell her that God did it again. He used a donkey to speak."

"You heard a donkey talk?" Missy asked, wide-eyed.

"No, sweetie, I *was* the donkey," Gregory thought he saw a faint smile suppressed on Melanie's lips. "Actually, the Bible uses an older word for donkey that would probably be more appropriate."

Melanie couldn't hide her giggles any more as she listened. Missy looked up at her, relieved.

"So, what happened?" Concern flickered over her face as she looked at Gregory.

"Nothing - yet. But whatever happens, it's ok." Gregory stood and shrugged.

"So, why did you come here? Just to gloat?" Melanie asked abruptly.

"No, not at all. Actually, I came because I really wanted to...encourage you. To go back to your dad."

Melanie's expression was unreadable. "That's impossible." She continued folding. "I don't have a car, and I can't walk there - it's a 10 hour flight. I'd need a plane ticket, and I can't afford one. Besides, I don't think it would go over very well."

"I think it will." Gregory smiled as he pushed his hands into his pockets.

"How do you know that?" She stopped folding and asked him, amused.

"Because I think that a man who would stand up for what he thinks is right, no matter what the cost, must have a real relationship with Jesus. It takes love to do that. Love that is stronger for others than for self." He smiled.

"But I - I can't just call him up and tell him to come get me," Melanie stuttered, trying to think of a plausible excuse.

"Why not?"

"I have a fleece," She looked at him with her familiar firm determination that told him argument was futile.

"Like Gideon." He replied.

"Yeah, kind of," She waivered," and my savings account… It will happen at the right time. I am surrendered to it."

"Ok." Gregory smiled.

"Ok then." They looked at each other for a while, smiling awkwardly. "Why do I feel like I won't see you again?" She said suddenly.

"I don't know. But you will always be in my prayers." Gregory replied sincerely.

"Thanks. You too."

Greg reached into his pocket and pulled out the little monkey from the coin machine and handed it to Missy. She squealed delightedly and showed it to her mom.

"The monkey! Thank you! Thank you!"
"She thought it was gone forever. How did you - ?"

Gregory shrugged, then showed her his pocket full of other toys from the machine. She laughed as he smiled and turned to go, waving at Missy who smiled and waved back.

~

It was late and nearly dark outside when Professor Schwarzerd finished grading his papers and gathered his things to leave. He locked his classroom door and began walking wearily down the empty halls, listening to the echo of his lone footsteps.

Just then, Dr. Ribera stepped from his classroom briskly. Tension suddenly filled the hall with its stifling presence as both men stiffened. Eying Professor Schwarzerd, the doctor looked down quickly and busied himself with his lock.

"Doctor," Professor Schwarzerd nodded a greeting as he passed.

"Professor." Dr. Ribera returned the greeting tersely as the professor continued walking. For a moment, the doctor considered receding back into his classroom to avoid having to feel obligated to walk with the Professor. He stole a glance in his direction.

"He looks so worn and tired," he thought to himself, *"Surely his influence and logic is flawed."* He smiled impishly to himself as he played the conversation out in his mind. Finally his pride got the better of him and he ventured a thrust as he called after the professor down the hall. "As a teacher of grace, your influence tends more toward legalism, you know." He turned back to his lock as the scheming smile still played on his lips. Doctor Ribera chose his words carefully as he relished the stirring conflict and continued. "There is therefore now no condemnation to them which are in Christ Jesus, who walk not after the flesh, but after the Spirit." He gathered his brief case and joined the Professor as he continued, "It is the *spirit* of the law we embody, for the law itself was nailed to the cross. We are no longer under the law, but grace."

Professor Schwarzerd stopped and waited for the doctor to join him, feeling a surge of energy flow through him at the thought of the opportunity he had been prayerfully waiting for. "It was Jesus that was nailed to the cross in our place, sir," the professor answered mildly, "For He is the embodiment of the law. The fact He kept the law in our place, and then died in our place, accepting the penalty of the law on our behalf establishes the immutability of the law. James 2:10 reads, 'for whosoever shall keep the whole law, and yet offend in one point, he is guilty of all' for we find that our life is not in harmony with the law. Yet, 'there is no condemnation for those who are in Christ Jesus', only because He has paid for our sin. The law itself is still there - unless you condone the breaking of the law...or is it just the one law you have something against? A man may say, Thou hast faith, and I have works: show me thy faith without thy works, and I will show thee my faith by my works, for faith, without works is dead."

"Therefore we conclude that a man is justified by faith without the deeds of the law. Romans 3:28." Doctor Ribera retorted, "Oh, but you teach the course on grace - if I'm not mistaken. So, you must know this already." He gloated in his perceived victory as he turned to walk the long way in the opposite direction down the hall toward the far exit in order to avoid having to walk with the professor to the parking lot.

Professor Schwarzerd looked thoughtfully after the little man retreating quickly down the hall. "Sheep or goat?" He asked quickly before the distance became too great. The doctor's pace slowed reluctantly. Professor Schwarzerd waited. The doctor stopped. What he thought would be a quick victory was turning into a discussion that he would rather not have. He preferred an audience, and was beginning to feel he had made a mistake engaging the professor without one. He turned to face the expectant professor slowly.

"I was unaware of your interest in zoology, Professor," he answered sardonically and turned to walk down the hall again.

"Sheep or goat, Doctor?" The professor pressed as he took a few steps toward him, inviting a response. "For the Good Shepherd divides His sheep from the goats."

The doctor halted his retreat and turned toward his

adversary warily. Then his face brightened as he recalled the passage the professor was referring to. Calculating his next move, he waited and let the professor join him. "Sheep, of course," he rattled off the verses, "'For I was an hungered, and ye gave me meat: I was thirsty, and ye gave me drink: I was a stranger, and ye took me in: naked, and ye clothed me: I was sick, and ye visited me: I was in prison, and ye came unto me.' So, professor, even in your inferred passage, the Word shows us what commends us to God - not the keeping of the law, but the essence of the law - love thy neighbor as thyself, and thy God with all thine heart. This is the law of the new testament, sir." He smiled graciously, certain that he was enlightening the professor.

The professor nodded graciously and continued, "I agree. However, I was actually thinking of a different passage - found in John 10, 'My sheep hear My voice, and I know them and are known of them.' in Matthew 7, Jesus said, 'Many will say to me in that day, Lord, Lord, have we not prophesied in thy name? and in thy name have cast out devils? and in thy name done many wonderful works? And then will I profess unto them, I never knew you: depart from me, ye that practice lawlessness.' Which law is He referring to, doctor?"

Sensing silence would be wise, the doctor replied, "Which law, professor?"

"The verse reads, 'Not every one that saith unto me, Lord, Lord, shall enter into the kingdom of heaven; but he that doeth the will of my Father which is in heaven.' What is the Father's will for us?"

The doctor turned taciturn as he walked the long corridors in silence. "You tell me," he grumbled.

"First Thessalonians 4:3 tells us 'for this is the will of God, even your sanctification.' Have you read much on sanctification?" The doctor shrugged and trudged on as the professor continued, "It's a fancy word used to explain the work God does in us as he creates the born again man of John 3:5-16 in us. Exodus 31:13 reads 'surely my Sabbaths you shall keep, for *it* is a sign between me and you throughout your generations that you may know that I am the Lord who sanctifies you.' It is a sign of allegiance, doctor, a sign that we are no longer in rebellion to God's word and His commands, that we acknowledge His rule and Kingship."

"God knows my heart, and that is all that counts," Doctor Ribera answered defensively. "I am a good man."

"Yes, you are. One of the finest I know. But it is not enough for God's standard. Charting our lives by mere human moralism is like navigating the seas without a compass. We must measure ourselves by God's standard alone. And His standard is the perfection of Christ. When we see ourselves in our true condition, wretched, miserable, poor, blind, and naked, then we can see our desperate need of Christ and His righteousness - our need of His precious and matchless grace imparted to us as we surrender ourselves to allow Him to live His life out within us. To acknowledge God's law is to acknowledge God as Sovereign. His kingdom of grace is filled with grateful subjects who know of the price for which they were paid."

The doctor checked his watch in agitation and

picked up his pace as he retorted, "Therefore a grateful heart would be the best evidence of salvation, don't you agree? One can feel it welling up inside as we contemplate His *grace* toward us."

The professor inclined his head graciously and continued very gently and tactfully. "Yes, there are times when our feelings for God are strong. But there are also times when He is very near, yet we feel alone, as when Jacob was wrestling with the angel by the river Jabbok, and Joshua was praying beside the Jordan, and Elijah was fleeing Jezabel. Our feelings cannot be trusted. Most particularly in these last days of earth's history - Jesus Himself asked if there would be found faith in the earth."

"And what do *you* propose then is the measure of our faith?" Doctor Ribera asked reluctantly, as he pressed on down the hall resolutely.

"When Jesus said 'I never *knew* you' to those who were pointing to their good works in His name, He was inferring recognition. He did not *recognize* the reflection of His character in them. In the beginning, He created us in His image. Through sin and disobedience that image was marred. He came to set us free from the law of sin and death, so that we can be free to obey his law of life, the law of love - for it explains how to love God and how to love our fellow man. As we allow Him to work in us to will and do His good pleasure, as we surrender to Him, He works in us to restore His image of love in us. Jesus said, 'if ye keep my commandments, ye shall abide in my love; even as I have kept my Father's commandments, and abide in his love. If you love me, keep my commandments.' With man, this is impossible. We cannot of ourselves keep any of God's commands. So when we do, it is the evidence of God working in us and willing us to do of His good pleasure. It is not the means of our salvation, but rather the sign that He is saving us. That is the miracle of grace in the heart, Doctor. That a man, dead in trespasses and sin, can be reborn anew, and now hate what he once loved and love what he once hated as his rebellious heart of stone is replaced with a soft, fleshy heart capable of true, selfless love. There is nothing on our part we can do to make this happen other than to *allow* God to do it in us - to surrender all, and fully accept His offer of salvation, for *this* is the true work of grace in the heart - that we will become like Him. Tell me, doctor, when you see Him face to face, will He recognize Himself in you?"

The doctor yearned to reach the exit at the end of the corridor so the conversation could end and they could part ways. His stocky legs had been churning as fast as he dared without letting his distress become too obvious, but the professor's longer stride had still reached the door first. He stood with his hand on the lever, eyes pleading as he waited for an answer. Doctor Ribera's eyes locked with his for a long moment.

"Excuse me, but I must grade these papers," Doctor Ribera pushed past Professor Schwarzerd and strutted into the parking lot.

Chapter 15

~ The Council Concedes

The reformers counseled quietly together around the large wooden table in the little anteroom beside the hall with the chairman presiding.

"I warned you they would come at us from this angle," Justus, one of the younger members of the group said passionately, "It is only logical that protesters of Rome should embrace all the Scriptures, including *all* the commandments of God."

"Keep the law?" a grey haired member retorted. "This reeks of legalism, Justus - it goes against everything Luther has been working to abolish!"

"Nonsense," Justus replied hotly, "The law declares

'thou shalt not kill'. Is it then legalism when I do not kill my wife and children each day? Or love? It is no more legalism when we *don't* do something God has forbidden than when we *do* something He has requested. Who are we to stand in defiance of one of God's express commands and put in its place a false sabbath - a tradition of men?"

"Let us not repeat Constantine's former mistake," another grey haired sage replied, sympathizing with Justus. "His compromise with Pagan Rome was intended to unify the crumbling empire, but rather it plunged all Christendom into this terrible peril."

"And what was tearing Rome apart? The very thing we face now - division!"

"Not division, truth, dear friend. He who called us is faithful to keep us. What of the faithful ones of the Alps who keep the Sabbath even today, in these perilous times?" The chairman spoke gently, bringing the group back to order.

"You mean the Albigenses and Waldenses? Shall we be hunted as they are?" An exasperated voice chimed in as tensions mounted.

"And others," Justus continued, "Even missionaries to barbaric Africa have returned with testimony of unreached tribes where the seventh day is kept! - no doubt converts of the disciple Thomas himself who died in their midst."

The chairman turned to Daniel 7:25 in his Bible and pointed to the Scripture. "The prophet Daniel declares the little horn 'thinks to change times and laws' - but he cannot change them, for the law is written in stone by God's own finger, and God has said, 'I change not'. Malachi 3:6."

One of the opposition shot a frustrated glance at the chairman as he found himself unable to defend his position.

"If the law could be changed, then Christ need not have died," the chairman reminded them gravely, "It is the *law* that demands the life of the sinner."

"There is therefore now no condemnation to them which are in Christ Jesus, who walk not after the flesh, but after the Spirit. For the law of the Spirit of life in Christ Jesus hath made me free from the law of sin and death." The opposition replied. He lifted his chin slightly, indignant.

"For what the law could not do, in that it was weak through the flesh, God sending his own Son in the likeness of sinful flesh, and for sin, condemned sin in the flesh: That the righteousness of the law might be fulfilled in us, who walk not after the flesh, but after the Spirit," the chairman answered. He was gentle, but firm.

"For by *grace* are ye saved through faith; and that not of yourselves: it is the gift of God: Not of works, lest any man should boast," a man with the thin, pointed nose speaking for the defense replied. His scanty grey beard quivered with each word.

"Do we then make void the law through faith? God forbid: yea, we establish the law," Justus replied earnestly. The strength of his youth punctuated his words as he continued energetically, "If ye love me, *keep* my commandments."

The two groups sat at odds, facing one another angrily. A grave older gentleman stood solemnly. "It is time to end the blood bath." He spoke with firm authority. "This is a small point to concede for peace with Rome. I move we accept the concession and make peace with Rome."

"God's law is not a small point." Justus leaned forward in his chair as he clenched his fist, his moist lips pressed together in a thin line.

"Think of all the souls we can reach with Scripture if we can just move with the sanction of Rome!" the man with the thin nose replied in a timid voice.

"They will burn you if you do not concede. Concession on this small point will bring peace enough to prosper our work - the message of salvation through grace! Surely a gracious God will overlook this one point!" The older gentleman's hands were raised as he pleaded for peace.

"He who offends in one point, offends in all. If we sin willfully after that we have received the knowledge of the truth, there remaineth no more sacrifice for sins, but a certain fearful looking for of judgment and fiery indignation, which shall devour the adversaries." Justus answered, unwavering. He stood with his arms folded over his scholar's robes,

The tired group looked expectantly at the chairman for his answer.

"As for me and my house, we will serve the Lord." The chairman answered slowly, reverently. He and those who agreed with him slowly left the room.

~

Back in the council room, a monkish priest dressed in the signature black robes of the black pope stepped forward to the throne where Pope Paul III was seated waiting for the council to return. The priest leaned forward and kissed his ring. The archbishop at his side leaned forward to speak to the man in black.

"And what does the illustrious Ignatius Loyola, head of the Society of Jesus, have to present to His Holiness, Pope Paul III?"

"His holiness is reminded that when I founded the order of the Jesuits, we vowed to end the heresy of the Reformation," Loyola answered.

"Yes, loyal son of the church," the pope answered.

"We have found a way." Loyola's eyes glittered under his dark brows. He stepped aside and two Jesuit priests stepped forward in their dark, significant dress. "This is our brilliant Spanish priest, Dr. Francisco Ribera, and Cardinal Robert Bellarmine of Rome."

The Pope looked expectantly at the men.

"Your Holiness will recall that it was the prophecies in Daniel and Revelation that gave impetus to the heretical movement," Dr. Francisco Ribera began respectfully.

"Go on, Doctor," Pope Paul III urged.

"What if the reformers are incorrect in their interpretation?" Francisco Ribera suggested mildly. The pope's interest was piqued. "What if the prophecies *don't* apply to the Church of Rome at all?" The pope stared at Loyola closely who smiled sinisterly and nodded his subservience as Ribera continued. "What if they point to...something or someone else?"

"Can you prove this?" The pope leaned forward eagerly.

"With time, I believe it can be done." Cardinal Robert Bellarmine bowed humbly with a self-satisfied smirk.

Pope Paul III chose his words carefully as he stood, "I commission you to explore this - *corrected* interpretation, my sons Ribera and Bellarmine."

Ribera kissed his ring as Bellarmine and Loyola knelt in obeisance.

~

The weary reformers comprised of both peasants and princes enter with their Bibles and take their place on the empty seats of the council. They are looked at with disdain by the papists who whisper amongst themselves and cast condescending glances at the newcomers.

"I believe the rest of the council is ready to convene, Your Holiness," Archbishop Reggio quietly informed Pope Paul III who seated himself authoritatively on his ornate throne.

"Proceed," replied the pope.

Chapter 16

~ The Time is at Hand

A small group of students gathered to study the Bible with Fitz in the dorm sitting room. They were surrounding themselves with pizza and sodas as Jeremy joined them, quietly in the background.

"I'm pulling up the 2,300 day timeline, the longest time period in the Bible, intact as one continuous prophecy, as it reads in the Bible, for those of you who want to have another look," Fitz said as the interest of all was turned to him. "And, a few other time prophecies that you might want to look at too," with a few quick keystrokes, Fitz pulled up more overlays onto the time charts he was using, displaying them through his projector on the wall of the sitting room. Gregory joined the group breathlessly, and a little late, from his meeting with

Melanie. Fitz nodded a greeting as the screen zoomed to the ending point of the 2300 days as he continued solemnly, "It all ends here - 1844."

"So, what's there? Nothing happened, did it?" A student holding a large, untouched piece of pizza asked.

"Maybe. Maybe not," Fitz answered, lacing his fingers behind his head as he leaned back with a loaded expression on his face. "But think about this - what if the whole Jewish religious calendar was actually one big time line?" Deftly he pulled up another animation of a circular calendar with the Jewish feasts marked on it and began to overlay and intertwine them over the timelines.

"Interesting concept..." replied the student holding the still untouched pizza, in the same awe as the others around him as the truths opened to their minds.

"Check this out -" Fitz zoomed into the center of the timeline where the cross was embedded and used his pointer, "Jesus died *on* Passover, as the antitypical Passover Lamb of God. And each of the other major events, like Pentecost, 50 days after the resurrection, happened exactly on time too."

"Ok," Gregory said, taking it all in slowly, thoughtfully.

"And, the next thing is the Judgment - the antitypical Day of Atonement, which began in the autumn of 1844." Fitz's illustration of a heavenly courtroom was brilliantly rendered. "Each case is to be decided, starting from righteous Abel to the last living professed Christian. And when the Judgment is complete, then Christ will come."

"That's actually the next thing that happens in every single one of those prophecies - judgment and then the end of the world," the student holding the pizza had finally taken a bite and answered with his mouth full.

"Yes - and *always* in that order," Fitz breezed through more of his amazing graphics as he illustrated, "Even our court systems today have a 2 part judgment, the first one sets the sentence, the second, the one that comes later, executes it."

"That makes sense," Jeremy spoke up from his dark corner, "because when Jesus comes again, He says He will give every man according to his works."

"Which would mean that He would have had to have decided what He was going to give everyone before He came." Gregory finished the thought.

"Exactly. So before Christ comes, all our cases will have been decided. There is no secret rapture and there is no second chance." Fitz said as he pulled up an amazing depiction of the second coming, and placed it at the end of the timeline. Then he used his pointer to drop an image of himself just before that. "And according to the Bible, we're right here, at the end of time."

"Yeah. Surrounded by a cloud of witnesses..." Another voice answered.

Gregory glanced at his Bible opened to the verse from Matthew 18:16: *in the mouth of two or three witnesses every word may be established.* "This is established by the word of way more than two," he breathed to himself as a solemn air fell over the students at the solemn thoughts going through all their minds.

"Makes you really want to get right with God, you know." Jeremy said quietly into the stillness.

"Because you love Him?" Fitz challenged gently, "or because you're scared?"

"Both maybe?" Jeremy smiled good naturedly.

"Yeah. I agree. I guess that's why God tells us to 'fear not' even to the end of the world." Fitz answered as he turned the lights back on, turned off his projector and started packing up his things. "More than ever we need to be out there, sharing the gospel."

Jeremy snorted with antipathy, involuntarily defensive at the familiar words, then he caught himself as all eyes turned on him. He shifted uneasily from foot to foot, not knowing how to recover from his obviously inappropriate response at such a solemn time. Especially considering who he was... He looked like he wished the wall would open up and hide him from the uncomprehending and judgmental gazes.

"You know, I used to really resent this computer when my dad gave it to me," Fitz cleared his throat, drawing everyone's attention back to him as he spoke cryptically. "I thought he was just humoring me when I told him I wanted to leave the animation and film industry and go into the ministry. I don't think he thought I'd stick with it this far into the game." He braved a steady look at Jeremy as he continued, "I used to think it was one or the other, serve God or animate. Now I think God is showing me through all this that He wants us to use every means to get the message of salvation out. No matter what field we find ourselves in, we need to be representatives for God."

"So, you think He gives us talents for a reason?" Jeremy asked, almost allowing himself a hint of relief.

Fitz smiled encouragingly as he turned the topic. "Yes I do. And I thought I'd make this whole thing into a movie or something. Maybe even have a small starring role in it."

"Sounds like a great idea!" Gregory replied excitedly as he helped wind some of Fitz's cables. "People will watch a movie a lot of times before they'd go to a Bible study."

"It would be tough to make a movie out of this! So much information..." Another student said as he started helping the others who were clearing the mess in the room.

"Yeah, you don't want it to sound too preachy," Jeremy agreed as he grabbed the small recycling bin and started pitching in the piles of soda cans that lay scattered around the room.

"Or put people to sleep! What would you call it?" someone else said.

"I don't know." Fitz paused as he zipped his projector case. "I was thinking something like 'The Mark of the Beast'."

Jeremy shook his head. "Too direct. How about 'Armageddon'?"

"Sounds like a Terminator movie," Gregory replied, "I like 'End of Days'."

"Now *that* sounds like a Terminator movie," Jeremy retorted, "it sounds like it's about the end of the world but it's about the end of the time prophecies. I think you should name it after Martin Luther."

"Yeah. I like that," Gregory agreed.

"Good idea," Fitz nodded excitedly, "We could call it 'Here I Stand', because that was his famous answer when he was told to retract his adherence to the Bible and the Bible only."

"I like that too!" Gregory agreed wholeheartedly. "Let us know if you ever get to make it, ok?"

"Yeah! I always wanted to be in a movie! How about you, Greg?" Jeremy answered enthusiastically.

"Naw," Gregory smiled, shaking his head. "I'd just like to watch it."

~

Professor Schwarzerd snuggled further down into his favorite comfortable chair, and adjusted the light shining over his shoulder. Books on the Reformation were stacked neatly on the table beside him, and in his hands was a large, worn volume on the life of Martin Luther. The sun streamed warmly through the window and his cat was curled in his lap taking a comfortable nap as he stroked her tangerine fur absently, lost in thought. He reached the last page and thoughtfully closed the book, pondering the profound meaning of what he was reading. He gently placed the sleepy cat on the floor and stood, quietly slipping the volume onto the shelf beside many other books on the Reformation, running his hands down the length of the shelf, trying to decide which one to read next. For a moment he hesitated over one marked "Early Reformers - Doctrine and Faith", then took it off the shelf and opened it to a bookmarked page with an illustration showing the seven-headed beast, and a little horn with a papal miter on his head. He traced the words of his handwritten notes beside the picture - "Rome". Turning back to his chair he settled down and opened the book to a dog-eared page. It was the chapter on the Council of Trent. His cat leaped back up onto his lap and settled down to continue her nap.

~

Pallavicini laughed again gently as he watched the remaining Reformers submit to the council's demands, and kneel before Pope Paul III. Slowly, they filed out subserviently under the pope's upheld blessing hand. As the last one left he cast a baleful look over his shoulder toward the gloating pope and Archbishop Reggio.

"Well done, Archbishop," the pope commended his orator when they were finally left alone.

Dr. Francisco Ribera and Cardinal Robert Bellarmine of Rome stepped forward mildly and kissed his ring, then stood back holding their rolls, smiling expectantly.

"Your holiness," the archbishop began, "Dr. Ribera has completed his studies and can report some excellent findings." The pope turned expectantly toward them.

"Your Holiness, we believe that the prophecies of Daniel and Revelation speak nothing of the Roman church," Cardinal Bellarmine said with raised eyebrows and a heavy accent, "but rather of one sinister man, the antichrist, who will appear at the end of time."

"You see, when Rome fell, prophecy...stopped. And will not start again, until after the rapture." Francisco Ribera postulated with an air of authority and grace.

The Pope's eyebrows raised in surprise, then furrowed, puzzled, as he replied, "But the rapture will end the world, - who will the antichrist oppress?"

"There will be a *secret* rapture, prior to the antichrist's appearance, that will only take those who are Christ's, and leave the rest behind." The pope rolled his eyes impatiently. Ribera responded firmly as he referred to his scrolls, "See, here in Scripture it declares that 'there were two men in the field, one was taken, the other left. Two women were grinding at the mill, one was taken, the other left'."

Pope Paul III waived his hand at them in disgust as he dismissed the thought. "The protestants will not believe you. They are too versed in the Scriptures and in prophecy. They know those verses refer to those taken to their destruction - those who are alive and remain are the Lord's. Even *I* know the word is plain regarding this point. Your... rearrangement of the dissections of Scriptures you are endeavoring to use will not prevail against them."

Patiently Ribera tapped his fingertips together as he offered his unyielding assurance, "In time, they *will* accept this new interpretation..." His dark eyes leveled firmly with the pope's as he continued, "when *we* teach in their universities, with authority. As for the rabble, we will entrance them with stories and fables. The theater, baird, and storyteller have always been an effective schoolmaster for educating the ignorant with our doctrines and beliefs."

"Compromise grows...like a weed, your Holiness," the Archbishop Reggio's lips curled almost into a sinister smile as he relished the memory of the prostrate heretics at his feet.

"And - it has taken root," Bellarmine's thickly accented voice lilted in his elation, "Once the novelty of the Scriptures has worn away, the people will return to their pursuits and amusements, and they will not be so versed in the Scriptures they profess to love as they are today."

"And we will be gentle as we lead them," Ribera lowered his eyes piously as he knelt at the pope's feet for a blessing.

Pope Paul III stood and crossed the penitent suppliants prostrated at his feet, "Like sheep to the slaughter."

~

"So, did you tell her what happened?" Jeremy pressed as he and Gregory headed back to the dorm after the Bible study.

"Yeah, how did you know?" Gregory answered, is eyebrows raised in surprise.

"Hunch," Jeremy shrugged. "What did she say?"

"That's not actually why I went to see her," Gregory was defensive, not wanting his friend to get the wrong impression.

"Sure," Jeremy condescended a little too quickly as he looked expectantly at Gregory. "So, what are you going to do now?"

"I don't know. My head is still spinning. I guess I'll just have to wait and see what God opens up."

"Are you going to publish your thesis?" Jeremy unlocked the door to the dorm and flopped down on his bed.

"Can't stop now, can I?"

Jeremy looked at him quietly, but said nothing.

"Hey, I meant to tell you earlier that I really appreciated your help in Dr. Ribera's class. I was surprised." Gregory said sincerely.

"I'm not all bad then, right?" Jeremy joked.

"Hey I didn't say that. But I think your dad would be proud." Gregory smiled earnestly.

"Well, I guess we'll find out won't we." Jeremy paused, not sure if he should say more, then opened up haltingly, "I applied to MechTech Aeronautics University."

"Really?! That's great!" Gregory's genuine esteem was comforting. "What did they say?"

Jeremy shrugged modestly, "They liked what they saw. I have the grades, I passed their tests..." He paused and blinked as if still not accepting the thoughts in his head and continued. "They offered me a full scholarship - but they require all their students to have pilot licenses."
"What?! I've never even heard of that!" Gregory moaned.

"Well, it's not out of the question. It makes sense, I mean, it is an aeronautics university, you know," he grabbed one of his flight magazines and started paging through it as if he didn't care.

"So, are you out? What's going to happen?"

Jeremy couldn't hold back a smug look as he slid his pilot's license up over the edge of the magazine he was pretending to be reading.

"No way! Is this thing real?" Gregory grabbed it and stared at it in excited disbelief. "How did you get a pilot's license? No one ever caught you off campus?"

"It is *so* hard to not do what you really want to do. Only problem is, they need 600 flying hours, and I'm short by...eight. And out of funds at the moment."

Gregory looked at him for a moment, then back at the license. Rubbing his chin, he handed it back to Jeremy and sat down on his bed. "I have a great idea. Are you allowed to fly out of state?"

~

Melanie and Missy gleefully boarded one of the small planes at Ace Flying School toting their small bundles of belongings. Jeremy turned to them from the pilot's seat with his headset on and gave them the thumbs up sign as the instructor closed the door behind them and locked it, then jumped into the co-pilot's seat next to Jeremy.

~

Gregory stood outside of the dean's office again, looking at Stanley Wilkinson's missing picture as he waited for the dean to call on him. Finally the dean's secretary opened the door and nodded to him to enter.

Nervously, Gregory seated himself in the chair across from the dean's large desk.

"Gregory?" Dean Bellarmine looked expectantly at him from over the dark frames of his glasses.

"Sir, I came to ask your permission to follow the Shepherd." Gregory tried to sound confident, but the crack in his voice betrayed him.

The dean appeared taken off guard a moment, then smiled condescendingly at Gregory's perceived weakness. "Excellent. Go right ahead," he smirked.

"Thank you, sir," relieved, Gregory stood to leave.

"That's not something you have to ask permission for, though, you know. This *is* a Christian college," The dean was obviously puzzled at the whole exercise.

"That's true, and I was hoping you'd say that," Gregory said as he remained standing.

The dean began to feel edgy, as if caught in a word trap. "Why?" he asked suspiciously.

"Because my thesis is really about following Jesus,

the good shepherd, sir," Gregory answered in what he hoped was brave tone of voice.

"No, it's not," the dean answered snidely. "It's about an old reformer's teachings that we no longer uphold as truth."

"You've read it?" Gregory feigned mild surprise.

"No - well, yes," The dean stuttered, nearly backtracking, then deciding on his course of attack "Well of course I've read it! You make my head spin with all your Bible quoting, preacher boy!" He slapped a crumpled copy of Gregory's thesis onto his desk with disdain. "Look, the Sabbath is just a symbol, ok? We keep the other nine commandments because they are good, the Sabbath one is just a symbol of the fact we keep it. Any one day in seven will do really."

"Then why would God be so specific about it?" Gregory countered logically, "Remember *the* Sabbath day - not *a* Sabbath day. He set it up as a memorial of creation, the day He rested. It's like saying just keep any day as your birthday or anniversary - you can't change it. It happened on a specific day."

"I think you are making a big deal out of nothing," the dean flailed his arms to encompass the air, "don't you know they changed the calendars and no one can know what day the Sabbath really was any way?"

"With all due respect, sir, I think trying to change God's law is a big deal," Gregory answered defensively, feeling his courage rising. "And they changed the dates, sir, dates only, not the days of the week, more than once too. For example when they went from the lunar calendar to the solar they added too many leap years, so the seasons and the festivals were off. In 1582 CE, Pope Gregory XIII ordered that Thursday, October 4 would be followed by Friday, October 15."

The dean flipped to a marked page and pointed to a highlighted section. "You said it is the same day as the day God rested at creation. The first Sabbath in Eden was thousands of years ago! We don't even know when it was. Things could have changed before they changed the calendars. Ever think of that?!"

"Are you saying that God can't protect His own law? The real Sabbath He started at the beginning was kept by His faithful people all through time - from Adam to Seth to Enoch, to Methuselah, Noah, Shem, to Abraham, Isaac, and Jacob, Joseph and Moses - check the dates for yourself on page 23, many of these guys could talk face to face, and nothing was lost." He leaned over the desk and pointed out overlapping age charts. "Even if it could be argued that it was lost during the Egyptian captivity, it was God Himself who reminded them which day it was."

"What do you mean?" Dean Bellarmine asked, allowing himself a moment of genuine interest.

"The Pharaoh said Moses had instructed 'the people to rest from their burdens' even before they left Egypt."

"Yeah, see, it *was* Moses' law, he must have picked the day," the dean countered.

"Well, the manna fell on all the days they were journeying in the wilderness, except the Sabbath. Moses didn't instruct God when to have the manna fall. And they were supposed to gather all they needed each day except the Sabbath. They had to gather twice as much on the previous day, and this was the only time the manna kept overnight. All the other days it bred worms and stank. Moses didn't do that either." The dean sat thoughtfully listening in spite of himself as Gregory sat back down in the chair and continued, "Through each Israelite captivity, God has always had a faithful remnant on earth that kept the original Sabbath - Daniel in the courts of Babylon, Ezra in Artaxerxes courts, Nehemiah, Jeremiah - Paul and the apostles worshiped and preached 'on the Sabbath days' in the synagogues, and with the Christian underground by the riverside and in the country. It wasn't until AD 321 that the church officially conceded to worship on Sunday on pain of death for slaves and loss of property for freemen, because of Emperor Constantine's 'Venerable Day of the Sun' decree, which was made to unify his crumbling empire." The dean regarded Gregory critically. "All my notes are documented with a ton of historical support."

For a moment Dean Bellarmine's face betrayed his vacillating mind. Shaking his head slightly as if to clear it he leaned back in his chair and rubbed his forehead, implying that Gregory was giving him a headache. He sighed as he eyed the now silent Gregory warily. "So you are determined to destroy this school and all it has stood for all these years in order to assert your theory? We will lose our alumni support *and* our grant because of your little pet research project." He hoped his manipulative angle would cut through Gregory's sound reasoning and go right to his heart.

"Would preaching Bible truth destroy a Christian school, sir?" Gregory's tone indicated that he stood firm in his position as he answered respectfully. "This is not new research, but a returning to the old. Maybe it's time the school turned back to the faith that kept its doors open all through the years that it taught truth. Following the Shepherd isn't easy, but He promised us that His grace is sufficient for us."

The dean stared disbelieving at his unwavering adversary as he closed the thesis paper indicating the interview had ended.

~

Somewhere later that day, hundreds of miles away in a modest suburban neighborhood, Jeremy watched from a waiting taxi as Melanie and Missy walked up to a neatly kept home and gave a tentative knock at the door. After a short wait, an older man, face filled with emotion, filled the doorway as he stood for a moment, blinking and unable to speak. Finally, as though he decided that words could never communicate the sentiments in his overflowing heart, he reached out and pulled Melanie into his arms, tears falling down his face, as he stroked the dark hair on the head of the little granddaughter he never knew he had. As Jeremy took the taxi back to the airstrip, tears of his own began springing up from a mysterious, hopeful well inside.

Chapter 17

~ The Ambush

Jeremy slipped furtively back into the school, tucking his flight cap into his jacket as he happily bopped down the hall with his iPod on. He moved stealthily past full class after full class feeling like a secret agent returning from a successful mission. Then suddenly the dean was standing in front of him. Jeremy nearly walked right into him because of the way he abruptly stepped in front of him.

"Oh, hey, Dean - sorry, I wasn't watching where I was going - " Jeremy stuttered, startled.

The dean smirked at him cruelly, "That's ok, Jeremy. I *always* watch where *you* are going." Jeremy squirmed uncomfortably beneath his hard stare. "Don't you need to see me in my office about something, Jeremy?" He asked manipulatively. Jeremy looked at him, puzzled but scared.

"Um - do I?"

The dean checked his watch mildly and continued as if Jeremy had requested to see him. "Sure, I have time to see you now. I always have time for the sons of the alumni. Especially those who have such important information to share with me, for the good of the school, of course. Right?"

Jeremy looked nervously around for someone to help him out of this trap, but the hallways were empty. He stammered, "But I'll be late for class - "

"I got you covered, Jer," The dean laid a firm hand on Jeremy's shoulder as he began herding him toward his office. "I *always* got you covered, don't I son?" Dean Bellarmine nonchalantly reached into his pocket and pulled out the business card from Jeremy's flight school instructor. Jeremy's face drained of all its color and his mouth ran dry. "Step into my office, son." He opened his office door and ushered a wordless and defeated Jeremy through.

~

Dr. Ribera stood just inside his class door as his students filed out. He stepped deliberately in Gregory's path as he tried to walk through the classroom door, barring him smoothly. "Oh, hello, Gregory," he smiled. Gregory stopped short to keep from running into Dr. Ribera. "I just wanted to remind you of something," Dr. Ribera continued calculatingly, relishing his power, " - something you might have forgotten in all your careful studies..."

"What is that, Dr. Ribera?" Gregory felt his concern rising as the students behind him whispered uneasily, witnessing the degradation.

"Well, in order to graduate," Dr. Ribera replied with mock nonchalance, "you do have to...pass my class, you understand, don't you?"

Gregory's brow furrowed as he watched Dr. Ribera smile at him again, slowly turn, and walk back into his classroom. Gregory stood, unsure of what to do as the other students pushed their way out the door around him.

~

Gregory sat in his desk chair miserably with his head in his hands. Jeremy sat back on his bed, leaning against the wall as he listened to his friend finish pouring out his troubles.

"So, he's not going to pass you, no matter how good a job you do, unless you change your paper so it agrees with his interpretation of prophecy." Jeremy recapped slowly.

"He didn't say those words, but I think that's what he meant," Gregory leaned back in his chair and stared at the ceiling.

"So, are you going to? So you can pass?" Jeremy tried not to let his tone sound too eager. Gregory leaned back on his bed thinking deeply, then shook his head and sat up.

"This is bigger than that. This is a battle I have to fight. What do you think I should do?" Gregory looked earnestly at his friend. Jeremy pulled his eyes away and started playing with his mp3 player.

"Well, for starters, if I were you, I think I would choose a new topic to write on," Jeremy winced as he caught Gregory's pained look.

"What! How can you say that? You know how important this is!"

"More important than wearing your graduation cap? Come on! This is serious! Your whole college career is hanging in the balance - I know you are sunk with student loans already, how are you going to pay them off if you can't even graduate?" Jeremy crossed his arms defensively as Gregory's face registered his frustration. Finally Gregory shrugged, defeated. "Besides Dr. Ribera already told you to change your topic over and over," Jeremy pressed, "even the dean told you to abandon your determined course to destroy the school. You have a lot of enemies."

Gregory looked darkly at his friend. "Destroy the school? Is that what you think I am trying to do? Is that all you think this is about? This is about the truth! Not the school!"

"Look, all I am saying is just graduate. Then go on your merry way, pastoring a church somewhere, and pick up your pet research project then. Ok?

Run from the battle today, and then you get to fight another day," Jeremy urged defensively. Gregory glared at his friend. Jeremy looked away and kept talking, trying to quiet his conscience by the sound of his own voice. "Besides, you're just all mixed up in your head because of that girl at the laundromat. Do you think you're going to help her and her dad get their honor back? They stripped him of his doctorate because of her - because she got pregnant. She brought all this on herself, now she's got this vendetta, and you're all caught up in it!"

Gregory exploded, "Is that what you think!? Is that what they told you? They didn't strip him of his doctorate because she got pregnant, her dad didn't even know about that! It was because of this teaching - he believed it too, and they kicked him out for that!"

Jeremy's face registered his momentary confusion. Catching himself he blurted, "Well, so? They will do the same to you, you know."

Gregory started pacing furiously as Jeremy fidgeted nervously. Suddenly Gregory stopped, thoughts registering on his face as he reviewed in his mind what his friend had just said. Staring hard at Jeremy he realized something wasn't right. Jeremy looked away and made himself small in his corner. "Who told you Melanie getting pregnant was the reason they disfellowshipped her dad?"

"You did," Jeremy's eyes flicked back and forth rapidly.

"No, I didn't." Gregory turned his cold, hard stare on him.

"Yes, you did. You must have. You tell me everything." Jeremy answered defensively, but his eyes betrayed him, as though he pleaded for Gregory to believe him.

"I didn't tell anybody." Gregory leveled his unrelenting gaze.

"Well, then I figured it out," Jeremy answered, trying to sound convincing, "Why wouldn't it be something like that? It was a good guess."

"You're lying to me." Gregory's soft words bit like steel as Jeremy cringed, "Whose side are you on anyway? I thought I could trust you! You're supposed to be my friend!"

"I *am* your friend, that's why I am trying to persuade you to save yourself and get out of their grip!" Jeremy suddenly stood up awkwardly and Gregory started pacing angrily, thinking. He stopped short abruptly and a look of concern crossed his face as he noticed his friend's suppressed distress.

"They turned you against me." Gregory informed himself out loud as his thoughts raced. "What did they do to you?"

Jeremy's face colored as Gregory's concern for him in spite of his spuriousness broke his will. "They threatened my scholarship. If I ask for a transfer, they won't give me any of my transcripts. I'd have to start all over! What am I supposed to do? It's hard enough to do this already without that!"

"I can't believe this! After everything we've been through together!" Gregory's exhaustion unleashed his suppressed anger.

"I'm sorry! I didn't know what to do! They said I had to help them convince you to quit or they would expel me. What about my family name!?" Jeremy answered angrily as they shouted at each other, red faced and emotions raging.

"Your family name!"

"We've had three generations of graduates from this college - do you realize what kind of pressure I'm under?"

"Three generations! - Is your family name more important than the truth?"

Jeremy suddenly looked away. Gregory caught himself and sighed, sinking down onto his bed, softening. "Jeremy, is your scholarship more important to you than *God's word*? Is what your family thinks of you more precious to you than the *truth*?"

"You don't understand. You don't know my dad." Jeremy masked the emotions that threatened again to crush him in anger as he turned toward the wall.

"Jeremy, whose approval means more to you - God's, or your dad's?" Jeremy was silent as he faced the wall. "You are going to have to choose who you worship." Gregory finished as he stood abruptly, grabbing his coat and Bible.

"Where are you going?" Jeremy demanded. Gregory stared at him in silence a moment, not sure whether or not to tell him. "Where are you going, Greg?" he pressed.

"I'm going to see Mr. James Todd." Gregory answered resolutely as he stormed out the door.

"The college president?!" Jeremy launched himself to the door after Gregory who was already striding down the hall. Jeremy ran his fingers through his hair in frustration as he slammed the door after him.

~

James Todd was sitting behind his desk sorting papers when his telecom buzzed.

"Yes," he pushed the ancient button and spoke into the machine.

"Mr. Gregory Martin here to see you, sir," Judy's voice spoke through the crackling speaker.

"Oh, how nice. Send him in," James Todd answered as he cleared his desk and took out Gregory's file. "Ready to register your new topic, are we Mr. Gregory... I'm sure Dr. Ribera would be happy to oblige." He chuckled to himself. "Good work, Jeremy. Your dad would be proud."

Gregory opened the door and entered the office

carrying his Bible. His face was hard and his jaw is set, but James Todd didn't notice as he gloated.

"Gregory, what a nice surprise. How can I help you, son?"

"Sir, do you love God?" Gregory was glad the long walk to the office had helped cool his thoughts. He wanted his mind efficient and he knew that if he spoke in anger or passion his arguments would lose their effectiveness.

"What kind of a question is that?" James Todd smirked.

"God's word says, 'If you love me, keep my commandments'." Gregory's voice was calm.

"So?" James Todd raised a haughty, questioning eyebrow.

"So, do you really love God if you don't want to do what He asks you to?" Gregory placed his Bible on the president's desk. "Or are you in rebellion to Him? A king can't rule when His subjects will not obey His commands. You show you are either on his side, by obeying him, or on the enemy's side, by disobedience."

"All or nothing." James Todd smiled as he leaned back in his chair.

"Yes." Gregory's face was sober.

"Please don't forget who the student is, Gregory Martin." The president's eyes were cold as he smiled again and gestured toward his many certificates on the wall.

"Respectfully, sir, I think rather I am learning who my God is." James Todd looked at him critically. He had underestimated him. "Mr. Todd, in my study recently I have come across two life changing verses that I now understand in a new light."

"Oh? And I suppose you would like to use these for your new thesis?" the president answered, pretending to be mildly surprised as he picked up his pen and waited, poised to write, "Well, I'm sure I can work out an extension of time for you with Dr. Ribera."

"Don't you even want to know what they are?" Gregory asked.

"Knowing your scholarly ability and your love of the Scriptures, I'm sure they will be appropriate," James Todd smiled triumphantly.

"Well, I'm going to tell you anyway." Gregory opened his Bible and set it on the desk in front of James Todd, pointing to the Scriptures and turning the pages for him to follow along. "Here in Matthew 10:32 to 34 it says 'Whosoever therefore shall confess me before men, him will I confess also before my Father which is in heaven. But whosoever shall deny me before men, him will I also deny before my Father which is in heaven'."

"Yes, yes, I see that. Interesting," James Todd was a little intimidated at Gregory's intrusion into his personal space and by his boldness, but his pride would not let him show it.

"Mr. Todd, sir, I will *not* deny my Lord, because I do *not* want Him to stand before His Father and deny me. I need Him more than life itself."

"Well, no one is asking you to deny the Lord Jesus, Gregory, we just want you to bend a little and adhere to the traditions we have always taught, and know and love. If you don't, you'll tear the school apart." James Todd hoped he sounded convincing as he endeavored vainly to reconcile the two irreconcilable positions in his mind.

"With all due respect, sir, you are teaching for doctrines the traditions of men," Gregory answered, suddenly realizing James Todd's ingrained, habitual capriciousness and misguided loyalty had rendered him nearly incapable of independent thought. Earnestly he continued, pointing to more verses, hoping he would let the truth set him free. "Look a little lower under those verses, in Matthew 10:34, sir. Jesus said, Think not that I am come to send peace on earth: I came not to send peace, but a sword." James Todd looked up over his reading glasses at Gregory blankly as Gregory continued, "*I* am not the one tearing the school apart, Mr. Todd. God's word is a sword and it is trying to cut you away from your adherence to a tradition that tramples on the Word of a Holy God."

James Todd leaned back in his chair and with a look of disgust on his face. "Do we have to go over this again?"

"A sword can defend or wound," Gregory continued, "depending on which side of the blade you are on. I want to be on God's side. If you are getting wounded, maybe you are on the wrong side of the blade."

"Leave the parables to Jesus, son," the president answered impatiently, "and tell me what your final decision is. We can't have you running rampant with your fanatical beliefs and ruining a school that has stood for generations. If you are not going to conform, I will have to take drastic measures."

"Which brings me to my next verse," Gregory pressed on as James Todd sighed deeply and rubbed his closed eyes, suppressing his annoyance. "It's here in Matthew 10 as well, just a few verses earlier. Jesus said to His followers 'whosoever shall not receive you, nor hear your words, when ye depart out of that house or city, shake off the dust of your feet. Verily I say unto you, It shall be more tolerable for the land of Sodom and Gomorrah in the day of judgment, than for that city'. Our God is merciful when we are seeking truth and learning, but when we know the truth and sell out, we've actually made the decision against God, and there is no more mercy. The choice is made. I've made my choice too. It's to stand on the side of the word of God. When He asks me in the judgment why I have taught what I have taught in His name, I will say, 'because You said so in Your Word, with Your own mouth, in Your never changing law'- not 'because my teacher or my pastor said so.' It's not too late, Mr. Todd. While you have life, you have a choice. I still hope you will choose to follow God's

Word as it stands." Gregory stared at James Todd with hopeful expectancy.

"Is that all, Mr. Gregory?" Mr. Todd crossed his arms and leaned back in his chair.

Gregory extended to him a typed piece of paper but James Todd did not reach for it. He simply looked at it mildly.

"This is my formal withdrawal from the school. I would appreciate a copy of my transcripts please." Gregory spoke solemnly.

James Todd leaned forward with a cold smile as he opened Gregory's file on his desk. "I'm afraid I can't do that, Mr. Gregory. You see, we can't complete transcripts for *expelled* students." He opened the folder slowly to reveal the top paperwork stamped with big red letters "EXPELLED". Gregory's face registered his utter frustration. "You see, your little illicit escapades with the laundry girl cost you quite a bit. You knew that she already had a reputation for being a little - shall we say, indiscreet. The board had no choice but to meet regarding the scandalous situation and determined it would be best for the reputation of the school to let you go. I'm afraid your request for withdrawal is too late. You won't be receiving any credit for the years you have spent with us. But you were warned. You brought this on yourself, Gregory Martin. I'm so sorry."

Gregory stared unbelieving at the paperwork on the desk. After regaining his composure, he turned and left wordlessly.

~

Mrs. Schwarzerd stepped up behind her husband as he was studying in his chair and wrapped her arms around his neck, kissing him on the cheek. "How is Gregory Martin?" Her soft voice was as warm as her presence in the room.

"I think he will pull through," the professor answered as he used the receipt for a bus ticket for a book mark and put his Reformation book on the stack beside his chair, pulling her around his chair and into his lap, smiling.

Chapter 18

~ The Victory

Gregory stood at the empty bus stop in the cold spring wind with his duffel bag at his feet, his Bible under his arm, and his laptop case slung over his shoulder. He watched as a lone, tall figure walked toward him, hands in his pockets, collar turned up against the cold.

"Hey. I wasn't sure you'd want to see me." Jeremy said softly as he reached his friend.

"Aw, you're still my friend. I just think there's still a lot of studying to do." Gregory smiled.

"Fitz's dad is calling a meeting of the alumni to study this out. It could go somewhere - maybe take over the college, or they could start their own college..." Jeremy's eyes wandered over the nearly deserted bus station as his voice trailed.

"That's great. I don't want to wait that long though."

"So, where are you going?"

"There's a missionary college of evangelism in California that has an accelerated teaching program and gets their graduates out into the mission field quickly. They listened to my story and said they would consider me on probation."

"Probation?" Jeremy tentatively jibed his friend, "It sounds like you just got out of jail or something."

"Yeah. Funny huh? It's hard for anyone to believe that I had all these years of study at a Bible college, and then got kicked out for wanting to preach the word. It just sounds corny. I won't get a doctorate or anything, but at least I'll be preaching. I don't want to start over. Jesus is coming so soon, I want to get out there and work for Him."

Jeremy stole a glance at his friend. Gregory was standing, facing the wind like a rock, but the familiar, fully accepting smile that revealed his true character still shined through. Jeremy looked down again as he shuffled his feet. "It would probably really help to have those transcripts, right? At least to show your grades and the courses you took..."

"Probably. But there's no way. So I'm just trusting in God to make a way without them." Gregory was fully at peace as he watched the clouds cross the sky as if moved by a powerful, unseen hand.

Jeremy reached under his flight jacket and pulled out a manila envelope. He stood holding it awkwardly, and then handed it to Gregory.

"What's this?" Gregory looked at him questioningly.

"Consider it a parting gift. I know they are not official, but at least it will back up your story some."

"How did you get this?" Gregory asked incredulously, opening the envelope and finding all his transcripts in his file.

"Well, I figured I was already breaking one commandment, I might as well break another before I repent," Jeremy replied jokingly.

Gregory shook his head, smiling at Jeremy's silly logic. Putting the file back into the envelope he looked at his friend squarely. "Thanks. I appreciate what you tried to do for me. But I really can't take these. If the Lord wants these in my hands, He'll give them to me without you having to steal them for me."

Jeremy shrugged as if he already knew what he would say. He accepted the file back. "Well, then if you need someone to vouch for you, I'd like if you called on me."

"Thanks." Gregory put an appreciative hand on his friend's shoulder. "I'll take you up on that. And I really hope you meant what you said." Jeremy tucked the envelope back it into his coat, listening thoughtfully. "I know it's not easy to make such a big change, go against the flow." Gregory handed his friend a piece of paper with a verse jotted on it. "This verse helped me a lot. It's my favorite. John 14:15."

"'If you love me, keep my commandments'. I know that one - you've said it enough by now for me to remember it!" Jeremy smiled. They laughed for a moment, then somberly said their goodbyes.

"You know God would never ask us to do something that was impossible, because nothing is impossible with God." Gregory beamed his winning smile at his friend as he gave him a hug.

"Pray for me. I'll be praying for you." They hugged each other briefly, then Jeremy slapped his friend on the shoulder and turned to go, disappearing into the crowd that began gathering as the time for the bus to arrive approached. Gregory sat down on the bench, flipping his Bible open, reading to himself out loud softly. "'He that loveth father or mother more than me is not worthy of me: and he that loveth son or daughter more than me is not worthy of me. And he that taketh not his cross, and followeth after me, is not worthy of me. He that findeth his life shall lose it: and he that loseth his life for my sake shall find it. He that receiveth you receiveth me, and he that receiveth me receiveth him that sent me. Matthew 10:37-40."

~

Late that night the janitor swept around a small group of students seated in the library, engrossed in a worn volume on the Reformation.

1521, Germany

A haughty prelate stood beside the emperor presiding over the Diet of Worms. Luther, alone and worn, was standing beside a table with his books and writings upon it. A large intimidating crowd comprised of nobility and world rulers, looked on expectantly.

"You have not answered the question put to you," the impatient Speaker of the Diet pressed, "You are required to give a clear and precise answer. Will you or will you not retract?"

Martin Luther lifted his weary eyes to meet the emperor's as he replied softly, but clearly. "Since your most serene majesty and your high mightinesses require from me a clear, simple, and precise answer, I will give you one, and it is this: I cannot submit my faith either to the pope or to the councils, because it is clear as the day that they have frequently erred and contradicted each other. Unless therefore I am convinced by the testimony of Scripture or by the clearest reasoning, unless I am persuaded by means of the passages I have quoted, and unless they thus render my conscience bound by the word of God, I cannot and I will not retract, for it is unsafe for a Christian to speak against his conscience. Here I stand, I can do no other; may God help me."

Epilogue

Gregory Martin graduated from the Mission College of Evangelism and is now in the field he loves, working with people, Bible studying with them, laughing, praying, leading mission trips, and sharing truth. A few years ago he graduated with cap and gown and scroll, receiving a doctorate from a college in southern Michigan, one of the many that teach the very truths he was expelled for believing.

He was there to shake hands with Jeremy, and pray with him as Jeremy left with his flight suit on for NASA's aeronautics division.

He was also finally able to put up letters on a marquee that reads "Gregory Martin, Pastor" at a church near Niles, Michigan.

His first sermon began with this testimony: "When the foundation of my faith was tested, and found to be nothing more than the mere suppositions of men, I wasn't sure how I could stand. But I found that God's word alone is my sure foundation - Here I stand, I can do no other. May God help me."

His favorite verse is found in Isaiah 58:12 "And they that shall be of thee shall build the old waste places: thou shalt raise up the foundations of many generations; and thou shalt be called, The repairer of the breach, The restorer of paths to dwell in."

Professor Schwarzerd took a position in another school. He has still not reached tenure, but he is still content and trusting God to continue to provide for him and his family.

Melanie and Missy are happy at home with her family and she still keeps in touch with Gregory.

Fitz is currently working part time at his father's animation firm and has just finished his first Christian feature film called "Here I Stand." Look for it online at www.hereistandthemovie.com.

Timeline

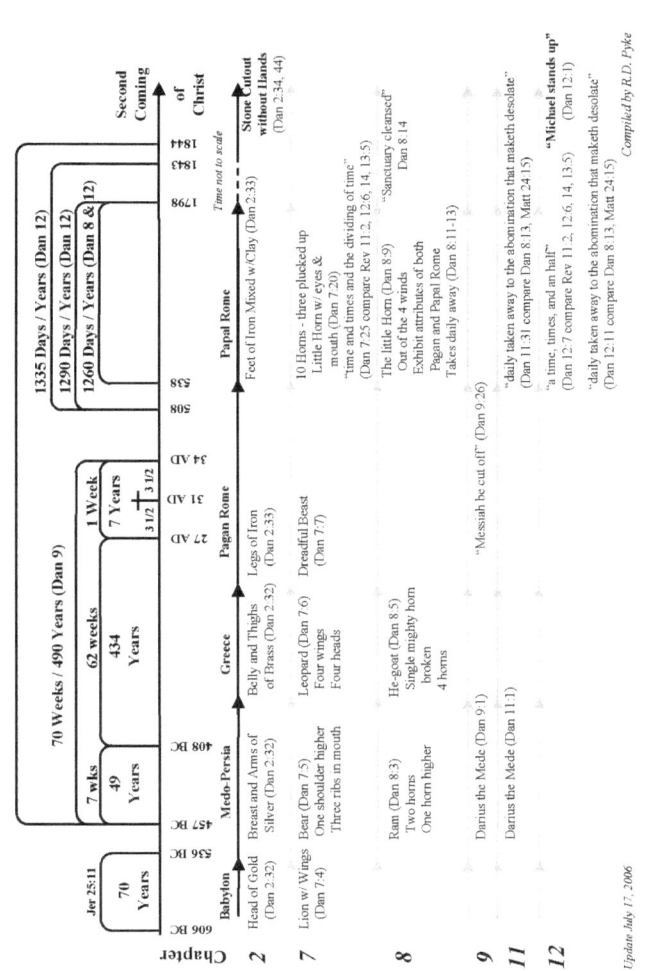

Daniel 2, 7-9, 11 &12

2300 Evenings and Mornings / Prophetic Years (Dan 8)

Compiled by R.D. Pyke

Update July 17, 2006

Visit the website for additional free study materials and resources:

www.hereistandthemovie.com

Look for more titles and works by Nicholas and Lauren Mazzio online at these locations:

Solemn Appeal
www.solemnappeal.com

Theater of Grace
www.theaterofgrace.com

The Luther Project
www.thelutherproject.com

The Rain
www.therain.com

Support this film and others like it by visiting

Watch and Pray Pictures
www.watchandpraypictures.com

Also available from Solemn Appeal Ministries:

The stirring true story of the life of Martin Luther, the champion of the reformation.
~ 3 CD audio book format.

The amazing and inspiring true story of the Hasel family, who dared to practice their faith in Hitler's Germany – no matter what the cost.
~ 6 CD audio book format.

Beloved hymns with a burst of color and depth to keep them fresh and alive because they are powerful and should never be forgotten.
~ Music CD audio

Brilliantly musical - Powerful lyrics supported by symphonic and powerful music.
~ Music CD audio

The scenes of Calvary, lovingly portrayed. Perfect for sharing or personal devotion.
~ Single CD audio book format.

The scenes of Gethsemane, thoughtfully revisited. Perfect for sharing or personal devotion.
~ Single CD audio book format.

The truth about God's Sabbath, lovingly presented. Perfect for sharing or personal devotion.
~ Single CD audio book format.

To learn more about these wonderful sharing resources, or to support this ministry, please visit:

Solemn Appeal Ministries
www.solemnappeal.com
888-449-1452

~ Notes ~

~ Notes ~